The Unrelenting

WRITTEN BY SUSAN PELTIER

CONTRIBUTIONS BY ELI ALLEN AND DAVID FONTENETTE

EDITED BY JEREMY HERMAN

"Anything that's human is mentionable, and anything that is mentionable can be more manageable. When we can talk about our feelings, they become less overwhelming, less upsetting, and less scary. The people we trust with that important talk can help us know that we are not alone."

— Fred Rogers

The Unrelenting

At the heart of the Midwest, tucked away in a forest on the outskirts of the Oregon Trail was a picturesque neighborhood, radiating with rustic charm. The roads were lined with maple trees and shaded by willows, while apple orchards blanketed the streets in sweet nostalgia. Sidewalks snaked through the houses, weaving stories of laughter and kindness into everyday life; children's giggles echoed in the warm air.

The thunderous toll of an old cast iron bell intertwined threads of inclusivity between neighbors. Its chimes came from Emily's great-grandfather's farm and marked significant times of the day, offering a sense of connection to everyone that called this place home.

Emily's parents—Jack and Alexandra—lit up every corner of their world. Jack, a much-admired entrepreneur, often chatted with locals in one of the local shops. He filled the room with his booming laughter as he shared tales from his latest ventures, earning him admiration from all who listened. Alexandra served as the heartbeat, her energy pouring out as she organized events or cheered loudly at football games. Her passion for their community inspired and uplifted everyone around her.

The couple's enthusiasm for life permeated their surroundings. They immersed themselves in their township's routines. Jack often spent his mornings at the river, casting a line and relishing the solitude of fishing. Alexandra thrived in the hustle and bustle of their dinner parties, filling the house with the chatter of friends and the clink of cutlery against plates. Whether listening to the soothing strum of a guitar or sharing heartfelt conversations with their friends, they cherished simple pleasures. They filled their weekends with activities reflecting the civic rhythm—bonfires flickering against the starry night and local parades that they always took part in, their vintage horse and carriage adding a whimsical touch.

During their dinner parties, Alexandra's laughter intertwined with the clinking cutlery and the chatter of friends. She wove through the crowd, pouring drinks and sharing stories, her eyes sparkling with delight. Jack, ever the gracious host, swapped stories with the men, his infectious laughter booming through the house as he made each guest feel special.

When wanderlust struck, Jack and Alexandra didn't have to travel far. Their explorations often took them to scenic towns or natural landmarks, their camper van offering a comfortable retreat while Jack steered along winding country roads. Alexandra marked points of interest on her map as she planned their itinerary. Whether visiting family, uncovering a new hiking trail, or simply enjoying a change of scenery, they treasured their weekend adventures. And each trip ended with their return to the familiar arms of their neighborhood.

More than just a house, their home pulsed with the stories and memories they shaped over the years. Carefully kept, each window gleamed in the sunshine, the white picket fence was always freshly painted, and the welcoming porch hosted countless hours of family time. This tranquil oasis stayed an integral part of the community, its doors always open to friends. Their children, Emily and Scott, matured in this environment. Their respectfulness and courteous manners were a tribute to their parents' guidance and the town's tight-knit values.

The heart of their home nurtured deepening family bonds each day. At the breakfast table, bathed in the warm morning light, they performed their daily ritual. Jack read snippets from the newspaper, sharing his thoughts and opinions, while Alexandra, coffee in hand, chimed in with witty remarks, provoking chuckles from Emily and Scott. This simple yet intimate routine served not just as a wakeup call but also reinforced their tight-knit bond.

The family's life unfolded like a treasured storybook. They cherished every moment together, from the hearty breakfasts in their kitchen's warmth to the Sunday picnics at the local park and the quiet evenings sharing stories on the porch. Their home extended beyond the beautiful house to the entire town, where everyone knew everyone, and each street corner and familiar face wove into the tapestry of their communal existence. Love and togetherness embodied the very essence of daily life, not just as words, but as a living reality.

Engrossed in a vivid daydream, Emily perched on a worn-out rug, her fingers clutching colored pencils. A jumble of discarded toys, strewn clothes, and crumpled papers littered her surroundings. Sunlight seeped through the hand-sewn curtains and cast a dappled pattern of shadows across her floor.

Emily worked furiously, breathing life into an otherworldly landscape. Every careful stroke of her pencils deepened the world taking shape on the paper. Emerald and sapphire trees, both in her imagination and the drawing, shimmered in the sunlight, their leaves rustling like hushed whispers. They towered over bodies of opalescent water, casting brilliant reflections. Riotous blooms sprouted around these trees, their sugary sweetness radiating through the air, warring against the mustiness of the room. Silken rivers flowed with enticing coolness, their tranquil murmur contrasting starkly with her silence.

Fantastical creatures of Emily's design roamed the scene— creatures half bird, half beast, their feathers hued with colors not found in the ordinary world. In the sky above, an assortment of celestial bodies twinkled, more than just a sun and a moon, but a constellation of radiant stars casting a kaleidoscope of colors onto the dreamlike tableau below.

Her mother's voice cut through Emily's thoughts. "Hey, Emily," she coaxed, "let's tackle this mess together. It could be a fun game. What do you think?"

Emily mumbled, her pencils hesitating as she kept drawing.

Her mother tried again. "Are you enjoying your coloring, sweetheart?"

Emily, lost in her thoughts, didn't respond.

Alexandra's patience began to wane. "Emily!" Her voice, heavy with irritation, resonated through the room. "Answer me!"

Flustered, she nodded.

Her mother held her ground in the doorway, her expectant gaze waiting for Emily's response. "I'm serious, Emily," she reiterated, "Clean up this mess!"

Setting her pencils aside with a sigh, Emily abandoned her drawings and rose to confront the reality of her disordered room. She started by gathering her toys - the teddy bears, action figures, and puzzles that had once been the centerpiece of her adventures. They found a new home in the large, wooden chest at the foot of her bed. Next, she picked up her clothes, scattered across the floor in various stages of wear and cleanliness. She sorted them into the laundry hamper and the closet.

Her attention then shifted to the wrinkled papers scattered across her room. Many of them were filled with sketches while the rest had half completed stories or random ideas that had once struck her as revolutionary. She straightened out each piece of paper and couldn't help but smile at the reminders of her imaginary journeys. These were placed in a special drawer of her desk, a treasure trove of creativity to revisit on another day.

As she continued cleaning, Emily's eyes often strayed back to her abandoned drawing. The colors seemed to dim without her attention, the world less vibrant. Yet with each item she put away, she felt a strange sense of satisfaction. However, once the last paper was tucked away, she glanced around her clean room. The concession made for her mother looked foreign and pristine, too perfect. She missed her comfortable chaos.

Emily's childhood was marked by adversity. She was born into a world where the smell of hospitals was more familiar than home. Her early years were spent battling constant illness. Her life was a study of resilience against an unseen adversary that drained her youthful energy.

"Jack, Alexandra, come sit down," began Dr. Vanier, the chief surgeon, his voice steady and calm, "I won't sugarcoat it. Emily's condition is deteriorating, and we're running out of time."

Alexandra swallowed, her voice shaky. "What can we do, doctor? There has to be something."

"There is one option left," Dr. Vanier said, pausing for a moment to ensure he had their full attention. "An exploratory surgery."

They clutched each other's hands.

"Exploratory?" Jack echoed, his brow furrowed in confusion. "You mean, you don't know what you're looking for?"

"We have some theories, but nothing concrete," the surgeon admitted, meeting Jack's gaze. "The idea is to get a look inside to understand what's causing her symptoms, and hopefully, treat it right there and then."

"It sounds risky," Alexandra murmured, her eyes full of concern. "Is it our only choice?"

"Unfortunately, yes," Dr. Vanier said softly. "With Emily's current condition and the lack of diagnostic results, this is our best shot at identifying and addressing the issue. I won't lie, it's a leap of faith. But it's one that could potentially save her life."

Faced with this harsh reality, Emily's parents exchanged a look that held more meaning than words could express. Their little girl was on the edge, and this was the only lifeline they were offered. With a deep breath, they turned back to the surgeon, their faces set with determination.

"When do we start, doctor?" Jack asked, holding Alexandra close, preparing to leap into the unknown for the sake of their daughter.

"First thing in the morning."

Beneath the harsh, fluorescent lights of the operating theater, the surgical team found an intruder nestled behind Emily's slender ribcage — a third kidney, a necrotic parasite, crowding her delicate internal structure. This malignant kidney was a remnant of abnormal development. Its mottled, purple, green-hued surface resembled a rotten plum, that starkly contrasted the surrounding healthy tissues.

There was a sense of preparedness among the surgeons. Their gloved hands moved with precision. The quiet beeping of the heart monitor punctuated the silence. They carefully excised the diseased organ from Emily's body. As the rogue kidney was finally removed, a collective sigh echoed from the surgical team.

In a deviation from the usual protocol, the doctor preserved the cut-out organ, a testament to the fragile boundary between normalcy and anomaly—a paradoxical symbol of both disease and survival. It was securely sealed in a jar and handed off to a nurse.

Emily was wheeled into the post-op recovery room. The overhead lights reflected off the clean, white sheets that draped over her, creating a halo around her peaceful face. Monitors attached to her kept an electronic vigil as she succumbed to a healing sleep.

Doctor Vanier, still garbed in his sterile scrubs, cradled the small jar in his hands. His heart pounded against his ribcage as he rehearsed the conversation in his mind. He understood the gravity of his role and the emotional payload the small jar held. Walking into the softly lit consultation room, he found Emily's parents, Alexandra and Jack, sitting side by side. Their faces were etched with worry and anticipation.

Alexandra asked anxiously, "Doctor, how did it go? Is Emily...?"

He held up the jar and calmly declared, "This was what was causing all the trouble."

Jack's face paled, his eyes widening with shock and a hint of revulsion. The sight of the organ was overwhelming. His legs trembled, his heart pounded in his ears, and for a moment, he teetered on the brink of fainting. Quickly, Doctor Vanier placed the jar down on the table, his eyes never leaving Jack's white face.

He reached out a hand, steadying Jack's shoulder with a firm yet comforting grip. With a deep breath, he explained, "This was her third kidney. It was necrotic and had been killing her. We've successfully removed it. Emily is out of surgery and recovering." His voice steady but tinged with relief, he said, "Your daughter is going to be okay."

Emily's path to recovery was a challenging one, requiring immense patience and persistence. She spent months in a world governed by medical routines, with a cycle of appointments, examinations, and endless tests. However, throughout this arduous journey, Emily clung to a glimmer of hope—the day she could leave the sterile hospital environment and return to the warmth and comfort of her home.

Finally, that day arrived, a mix of jubilation and slight anxiety. Stepping through the front door, she felt a rush of excitement. She was greeted not only by familiar sights and sounds but also by a deep sense of freedom. Her legs, still frail, could now explore the green grass of the backyard.

"Can we go outside? I want to run!" Emily exclaimed excitedly.

Jack replied with cautious encouragement, his voice filled with a mix of support and caution, "Take it slow. Your body is still healing. One step at a time, and soon you'll be racing through the yard."

Physically, Emily stayed the size of a two-year-old, her growth stunted by her illness. The disease had not only affected her physically but also robbed her of precious moments of her childhood. Now, she had to relearn those lost skills, akin to a toddler taking her first steps. She began by crawling, her hands and knees becoming familiar with the sensation of movement. Her body still kept memories of her earlier ailment, causing her legs to falter in her first attempts. She would start off, only to stumble and fall repeatedly.

Watching these attempts anxiously was her father. Each time Emily stumbled, Jack would rush to her side, his heart burdened by the fear of her getting hurt. Yet, she would look up at him with determined eyes, reassuring him that she was all right.

"Emily, are you okay? Did you hurt yourself?" Jack's voice was filled with concern as he knelt beside her.

"I'm ok," she replied, a small smile gracing her face. "Just a little stumble. Can I try again?"

"Sure, sweetheart," Alexandra chimed in.

As time passed, Emily's determination grew stronger. Her crawling became faster and more stable, eventually giving way to tentative steps. The first attempts were shaky, her small frame swaying precariously, but with each passing day, her steps became more confident. It was a slow and gradual journey, but with persistence, she finally learned to run. This physical transformation mirrored a profound shift within Emily, leaving an indelible mark on her emotional well-being.

Her once infectious laughter faded, replaced by extended periods of silence, occasionally interrupted by the sound of her pencils gracefully gliding across paper. Despite her longing for outdoor play and genuine friendships, her attempts to interact with others were met with stares and mocking comments, leaving her feeling rejected and isolated.

The neighborhood children were quick to notice that she was different. Their unfiltered perceptions made her an easy target for ridicule in the relentless world of playground politics. She had become sensitive, and the hurtful comments and gestures further deepened her sense of isolation.

Within her loneliness, Emily found consolation and refuge from the unkind outside world. As she withdrew into her own thoughts, embracing the silence, her imagination flourished. The blank pages transformed into a sanctuary, an infinite canvas where her dreams could unfold without constraints. Through her pencils' strokes, she poured out her innermost emotions and gave shape to her deepest desires. The realm of creativity became her escape, allowing her to transcend the limitations of her circumstances and construct a reality entirely of her own making.

Alexandra captivated those around her. Her vibrant energy tirelessly painted an illusion of flawlessness around their home. She created a serene, picture-perfect existence for her family. Beneath this manicured facade, she harbored uncertainty, fretting over her neighbors' opinions. Imagined whispers and perceived judgments often consumed her.

Despite her profound love for Emily and Scott, her responsibilities sometimes overwhelmed her.

"I know things are tough right now," she said, her hand gently combing through Emily's hair. "It's going to work out. We'll be ok. You, me, and your brother—we're a team. Right?"

When her children's liveliness drew attention, she felt embarrassment creep in. "Do you think the kids were a bit too loud at the picnic today, Alexandra?" Jack asked, concern in his eyes.

"Yes, Jack. They're energetic kids, aren't they?" she replied, forcing a smile.

Alexandra appeared self-assured, but beneath her radiant smile hid a whisper of self-doubt her socially graceful armor couldn't conceal. Feelings of inadequacy gnawed at her, continually making her question her worth. It was during such moments that Jack's reassurance shined through.

"You're doing a terrific job, Alex. You know that, don't you?"

Driven by a desire to please and a yearning to stand out, she relentlessly pursued her responsibilities with fervor. She craved validation and wanted to overcome her insecurities. However, her pursuits often isolated her.

Given the demanding nature of Jack's work life, his presence at home was sporadic and unpredictable. His commitments, critical meetings running late into the night, last-minute business trips, and the never-ending paperwork often meant that he was more a guest in his own house than a resident. This continuous cycle of his professional demands left Alexandra alone to manage their activities.

From mundane chores like tidying the house, managing bills, and preparing meals, to more significant responsibilities like attending parent-teacher meetings and ensuring their social calendar was up to date, she found herself shouldering the weight of their life alone. The burden was not just about the physical tasks, but also the emotional toll it took on her to keep their life running smoothly in his absence. Her days were filled with the silent echoes of Jack's nonattendance, and her nights were filled with the solitary company of her own thoughts, underscoring the magnitude of her isolation during their shared life. She longed for companionship and the comforting warmth of love that turned a house into a home.

Each night, when Jack returned, she voiced her feelings under their bedroom's soft glow. "I miss you, Jack. Everything feels better when you are home."

The relationship between Emily and her brother Scott was complicated. Scott could be both protective and cruel, leaving Emily conflicted.

"Hey, Emily." Scott offered a small toy. "Play with this." His gentleness was as fleeting as was rare. Moments later, he snatched it back, a smirk and a wicked gleam in his eyes. "Too bad you're so slow," he scoffed, his tone contrasting sharply with the softness he displayed just moments before.

Emily craved her older brother's affection despite his unpredictable behavior. His actions, both caring and cruel, often left her confused and longing for consistency. On some days he was her guardian, shielding her, while on others, he would vent his frustrations on her, his anger as painful as physical blows.

Scott was a study in contrast. The all-American boy image—handsome, charismatic, and impressively skilled on the football field—contrasted with a storm of anger brewing beneath. He relished being the golden boy, the apple of his parent's eyes. His energy and agility shone on the football field. He savored every touchdown, every victory stoking his desire for paternal pride.

"Dad, did you see that last touchdown? Man, that felt good!" he bragged to his father after a football game, his eyes gleaming with excitement and approval.

But his attitude changed when he thought about his sister. A shadow of malice crept into his sunlit demeanor. Teasing Emily was his preferred pastime, a brutish diversion that brought a disturbing glint to his eyes. An undercurrent of envy surged through him every time their parents' attention fell on her.

"Oh, look at our little Emily. Isn't she adorable?" He mocked his parents in a whiny, mocking tone, his jealousy showing.

His taunts were ruthless. The names he called her were brutal.

"Emily, why do you always have to be such a piece of shit? What an asshole," he said with disdain, his words sharp as a knife.

But these bitter interactions were private, saved for when they were alone. "Emily, you know I'm just messing with you, right?" He tried to reassure her later, but his attempt to smooth things over felt insincere.

In the presence of strangers, Scott wore a mask of polished civility. His manners were impeccable, personifying a good upbringing. But Emily could see through the veneer. Beneath the practiced smiles and courteous nods lurked something malevolent, a cold malice that chilled her to the bone. Despite the charm he wielded like a weapon, she could never shake the sense of foreboding that tinged her interactions with him.

Still, Scott's complexity confounded her. His temperament wavered between vindictiveness and protective affection, often leaving her disoriented. There were moments when his brotherly instincts overruled his cruelty. He would unexpectedly defend her, warding off potential threats with a fierce intensity that surprised even him.

"Stay away from my sister. Got it?" He warned one boy at their school, his voice filled with protective intensity. During these rare instances, Emily saw a glimpse of the brother she wished he could always be, a tender counterpoint to his usual abrasiveness.

Strung tightly to his explosive nature was an inexplicable fear. For a twelve-year-old boy, his dread often manifested in puzzling and distressing ways, creating unsettling situations far removed from typical childhood fears.

"Why can't you be normal, Emily? You're always scared of everything. It makes me hate you!" His fear-filled voice confused Emily even more.

One tense afternoon, Emily experienced a vulnerability she had never anticipated. She was playing when Scott stormed into her room and seized her. His cold, unyielding grip closed around her bare arm, and he dragged her roughly through their house along an infinite path. She resisted, but this only served to fan his anger.

"Let go of me, Scott!" she protested, her voice quivering with terror and defiance, punctuating gasps and strained breaths, as she struggled to free herself.

"Shut up, you worthless piece of shit!" Scott retaliated, yanking her hair and tightening his grip.

He was indifferent to her pleas. Emily's cries evolved into primal screams of fear as she strained against his relentless hold. "You asshole! Let me go! I hate you!"

The gritty wood beneath her feet and the chill from the night air signified their approach to the front door. A shudder ran down her spine, intensified by her fear.

The shrill scrape of the front door wrenching open made her breath hitch in her throat. Scott shoved her outside. The intensity of her vulnerability hit her like a physical blow, the frigid air raising goosebumps on her bare skin. The rough concrete under her bare feet, the taste of panic-heavy saliva in her mouth, and the deafening silence of the night around her, all magnified the terrifying reality of her situation.

The metallic click of the door lock sounded devastatingly loud in the stillness, like the final verdict of her abandonment. The sound echoed in her ears, pulsating in sync with her pounding heart. She pounded on the door, her pleas for reentry swallowed up by the oppressive silence.

Fear gave way to humiliation, her tears intensifying the raw chill against her bare skin. The afternoon air, usually warmed by the sun and perfumed with blooming flowers and fresh grass, now felt icy and sterile. Each cry scraped against her throat, her voice trembling and cracking under the strain.

"Why can't you just leave me alone, Scott?" Her plea echoed hollowly against their home's walls as she pounded on the door in rhythm with her racing heart. His laughter mocked her from behind the locked door, a disturbing celebration of his cruel triumph.

A man across the street watched the entire spectacle with unnerving curiosity. His eyes held no concern for her plight, just the cold curiosity of a bystander mesmerized by the unfolding drama. His indifferent nod pierced her chest.

Stripped of her dignity and exposed to his indifferent gaze, she sought the scant shelter in the nearby bushes. Naked and vulnerable, her mind was a whirl of uncertainty.

When the door finally unlocked, a rush of relief almost buckled her knees. But fear and humiliating shame clung to her like a second skin. The neighbor's stern voice cut through the night, forcing Scott to face the consequences of his actions.

"You think this is funny, Scott? Locking your sister out like this?" Their neighbor reprimanded him, disapproval clear in her voice. But the damage was already done. Emily understood her brother had violated her and she was helpless to protect herself.

These painful episodes hardened into a grim routine, dulling her senses until she simply accepted the degradations as a regular part of her life. She moved through each day under a cloak of anxiety, tiptoeing around Scott to suppress his explosive rage. However, the eggshells that she so carefully walked on seemed to shatter at the slightest provocation, setting off his wrath with an unsettling frequency.

She begged her mother to intervene.

"Mom, please, you need to do something. Scott... he scares me," Emily implored her mother one day, desperation weighing heavily in her voice. But what scared her more was not just Scott's anger, but also his growing paranoia. She had noticed him staring out into the dark as if expecting danger to appear from the shadows.

Her pleas, however, met with deaf ears. Alexandra brushed off her panic as an overblown reaction, misconstruing it as a typical sibling rivalry.

"You're just overreacting, Emily. Scott wouldn't hurt you," her mother retorted, irritation clear in her tone, disregarding Emily's fear as an exaggerated response to what she saw as typical sibling dynamics.

Scott, as the favored son, always enjoyed the benefit of the doubt. In her mother's eyes, he could do no wrong, leaving Emily trapped in an agonizing cycle of fear and pain.

Yet, his fear kept growing, his glances out the window becoming more frequent. Something was lurking in the shadows, something only he seemed to perceive. And Emily knew one day they would have to face it."

That day came sooner than Emily ever expected.

Fear took hold of Scott. Wide-eyed and trembling, he grabbed Emily's hand, and they started gathering every firearm and knife. The dimly lit bedroom was casting eerie shadows that harbored hidden dangers. The faulty lock on the window, an insignificant detail they had always overlooked, now seeded growing terror within them. Despite his shaking hands, Scott displayed firm determination. A belief had rooted itself in his mind - an unknown intruder, a man with murderous intent, was about to break into their home.

"Emily, we have to hide. He's coming! I can feel it," he whispered to her, his voice trembling.

"Who's coming?" Emily questioned, her heart pounding harder as she remembered the strange man who had been watching her from across the street when Scott had locked her outside.

"Just do what I tell you," Scott ordered, his teeth gritted with desperation Emily had never seen before. His eyes flamed with a mix of fear and determination that sent a shiver down her spine.

"Scott, what are we..." Emily began, but the urgency in Scott's eyes silenced her.

"Just shut up and do what I tell you. Help me with the dresser." His terse command echoed in the room, the gravity of his tone compelling Emily to immediate action.

They were in their jack and Alexandra's bedroom, heaving the heavy wooden dresser across the floor. Its legs scraped against the hardwood, the jarring sound carving its mark into the silence of the house. As they pushed it against the door, Scott's face was taut with strain, sweat trickling down his forehead.

In response to his unspoken plea, Emily darted across the room, throwing her effort into moving their queen-sized mattress. The weight of it surprised her, demanding her to dig deep for strength she wasn't sure she had.

"Is this... really necessary?" Emily managed to ask.

"Just do it! Please," Scott responded, his voice laced with a worry that spurred her into continuing.

They lifted the mattress, leaning it against the dresser-blocked door. Their fortress was makeshift and rough, but it added an extra layer of security.

Gasping for breath, Scott turned to Emily, the intensity in his gaze stealing her breath.

He handed her a rifle, his voice a husky whisper in the thick silence of the room, "Take this, Emily. Stay close to me."

The unexpected coldness of the weapon startled her, drawing a gasp from her lips. She looked up, her eyes meeting Scott's. The fear mirrored in them both was a chilling confirmation of the reality they were in. Emily swallowed hard, clutching the rifle closer.

"I'm scared, Scott," she admitted, her voice trembling.

The night dragged on, their shared fear vibrating through the silent house, each creak, each rustle outside amplifying their fear. Time seemed to stand still as they listened intently for any sign of danger. Scott's composure crumbled, revealing a terrified boy beneath his tough exterior. Emily sat beside him, her hand tightly clutching the rifle, her mind filled with a million horrifying scenarios.

Suddenly, a faint sound pricked Scott's ears— their German Shepherd's growl from the kitchen.

"Stay put," he whispered urgently to Emily before venturing into the darkness beyond their room, his father's rifle firm in his grasp.

Left alone in the room, Emily was a statue of tension and fear, her body rigid, and her senses hyper-alert. Their German Shepherd's unusual restlessness in the past week, which they had shrugged off, now seemed like a grim sign that Scott's fear was real. Each deep snarl sent waves of adrenaline ricocheting through her. Every tiny noise was magnified. The creaks and groans of the old building sounded ominously loud in the oppressive silence.

She strained to pick out specific sounds, her breath held as she focused intently, her ears attuned to the smallest noise. However, the pulsating rhythm of her own heartbeat was consuming, a thunderous soundtrack to her terror that threatened to drown out everything else. It pounded in her ears, echoing her fear with each heavy beat, creating an intrusive backdrop to the dire situation.

In her mind, terrifying scenarios played out one after another. She imagined shadowy figures creeping through their home, intruders brandishing weapons, their intentions malevolent. Each new possibility terrified her more than the last, and with each passing second, fear grew, coiling in her stomach like a venomous snake ready to strike.

Suddenly, the alarming sound of metal clattering against the floor and the sliding back door slammed shut, shattering the tense silence. It was a loud, jarring noise that caused her already rapid heartbeat to stutter in her chest. A chill of pure terror swept through her, washing over her in a bone-deep wave that left her feeling cold despite the clammy sheen of sweat covering her body.

Scott's scream was a raw, unfiltered panic, a sound that no protective older brother should ever make. The echo of his scream seemed to vibrate through the house, sending a jolt of alarm coursing through Emily.

She heard rapid footsteps pounding against the wooden floor, growing louder as they neared. The door swung open with such force that it crashed against the wall, and Scott rushed in. He was panting heavily, his face pale and stricken with terror, as he pulled their still-growling dog in behind him. Without a word, he kicked the door shut, the sound reverberating through the silent room and marking the end of his terrifying encounter.

"He tried to grab me, Em. I don't know who he was or what he wanted, but he's out there," Scott confessed, his voice shaking, his face pale from the encounter.

Emily listened, her heart pounding in her chest. The raw fear emanating from him was chilling, and she realized then just how truly alone they were. With their mother gone and a perceived threat looming over them, they were left to face the dark unknown by themselves.

In the heart-stopping silence that followed, they huddled together in shared fear and waited - for their parents' return or for the anticipated attack. The ticking of the clock on the wall seemed to mock their fear, each tick-tock echoing in the tension-filled room.

As their parents returned, they found their home resembling a battlefield mess. Furniture lay haphazardly tossed aside, and firearms were scattered about, silent testimony to the terrifying experience Emily and Scott had endured.

"What the hell have you two been doing?!" Jack's booming voice filled the house, a storm interrupting the momentary relief after their shared horror.

Seeing his meticulously maintained firearms strewn haphazardly unnerved him. The sight of his children disregarding these rules, so thoughtlessly, ignited a fury within him. He couldn't bear to think about the potential harm they might have inflicted upon themselves, or worse, on each other.

In response to his reaction, Emily and Scott rushed to justify their actions. Their words collided, tripping over each other in a desperate bid to explain the state of the house. They spoke of their fears, the strange man across the street, their constant worry, and the unexplained noises that had forced them into such extreme actions.

"Dad, we heard strange noises and footsteps... and the dog was growling..." Emily's stuttered explanation was punctuated by her nervously twisting fingers.

"And the guy tried to grab me, Dad! We weren't playing!" Scott chimed in.

Their father met their frantic explanations with deep skepticism. He cast a doubtful eye over their far-fetched tales. Given their history of overactive imaginations and tendency to dramatize minor incidents, their claims did not convince him.

"Scott, did you actually see anyone?" Jack questioned, his eyes blazing with anger.

"Not exactly, but..." Scott's explanation was abruptly interrupted.

Jack's stern gaze surveyed them before he spoke, "Guns are not toys. And this..." he gestured broadly to the chaos around them, "...is unacceptable. If there was any actual danger, all this chaos would have just announced your presence to anyone wanting to harm you."

Jack's frustration boiled over as he imagined his children panicking needlessly and creating havoc over a potentially harmless situation.

"Bed. Now," he ordered, directing a stern finger toward the door.

His sharp rebuke, combined with their lingering fear, created a contradictory atmosphere. To him, this incident seemed like a catastrophic fallout of a reckless game. But to Emily and Scott, it was a bone-chilling brush with a potential nightmare. Their father's disappointment, on top of the haunting image of their wrecked bedroom, left them feeling more isolated than they had during the silent terror of the night.

Emily's father was a towering, slender figure. His hair was dark and cropped short, complemented by a neatly trimmed beard that he wore with pride. His deep-set black eyes were imposing and captivating. On his right hand, an imposing Masonic ring glinted gold, a testament to his allegiance and amplification of his commanding presence.

"It's better if we just stay out of his way," her mother whispered in a warning.

He alternated between periods of stifling silence and explosive tantrums, holding everyone in a state of constant alarm. His presence loomed like an impending thunderstorm, his disruptive behavior denying any attempts at routine or stability. His brooding silences, even during his quiet phases, hung heavily, a silent countdown to an outburst that could come without warning.

Despite their best efforts to appease him and keep calm, they often found themselves at the receiving end of his unpredictable mental state. His disruptive behavior thwarted any attempts to establish routine or stability. They knew their only choice was to remain inconspicuous. Her mother's fierce love failed to protect them.

To deal with this, Emily took refuge in her imagination, creating a fantasy world to escape her fears and uncertainties.

When night fell and shadows deepened, the unbearable silence forced Emily to close her eyes tightly. She concentrated all her thoughts on the tiny space between her thumb and forefinger, believing she could slip into it and hide. Gradually, the surrounding room vanished, replaced by the smell of fresh-baked cookies and the soothing sounds of birds.

Her mind fell back onto the soft grass, cushioning her as she lay in a sun-dappled clearing where time froze, and troubles melted away. Safe from her fears, she felt unreachable as long as she remained focused.

Jack usually arrived home late each night. His late returns had become a routine part of their daily lives. He concealed his addiction underneath the facade of a hardworking family man, his outward persona hiding his inner turmoil.

His evenings began with a weary slump onto the dinner table, where a meal carefully prepared by Emily's mother awaited him.

"Dinner's ready, Jack. How was your day?" his wife asked softly.

Jack and Alexandra talked about the day's events, their hushed voices providing a calm soundtrack to the meal. Emily, however, navigated this space with heightened awareness, trying her best to remain unseen.

"Emily, finish the food on your plate," her mother urged quietly.

Emily understood the precarious nature of her father's temperament, where a single misstep might spark an explosion of rage. A plate not emptied, an unexpected request for a second helping—such minor things could tip the balance. Her father would erupt in frustration.

"For God's sake, Emily! Can't you do anything right?"

During these outbursts, her mother retreated into stillness, becoming a silent observer of her husband's rage. These tense, quiet meals set the tone, injecting an unnerving silence into their otherwise ordinary suburban life.

Emily sought refuge in her mother during these moments, a silent cry for intervention.

"Mom… please," she pleaded quietly.

But her appeals always met her mother's impassive face, an immovable stone wall offering no support or comfort. She learned a harsh lesson early on—when her father's fury unleashed, she was alone to fend for herself.

During these tense moments, an unsettling undercurrent appeared. Emily's mother, usually apathetic and still in the face of Jack's rage, showed an inexplicable glint of satisfaction when Emily became the target of his wrath. These faint but present flashes added a disconcerting layer to an already complex family dynamic.

One evening, when Emily's father arrived home late, her mother remarked flatly, "Dinner's cold, Jack."

"So?" Jack retorted; his words tinged with irritation.

From her room, Emily heard the murmur of his conversation with her mother in the kitchen. Suddenly, his voice, louder and angrier, sliced through the peace of the evening. A loud crash made Emily jump.

"Dammit! Can't you do anything without making a mess?" Jack barked.

"I'm trying, Jack! Just calm down!" Her mother's pleas echoed with frustration and fear.

The sound of scuffling, followed by what seemed like a hurried cleanup effort, reached her ears, interrupted by her father's sharp order.

"Dammit, Alexandra, just leave it," he ordered, authority ringing in his voice.

Glass shattered somewhere, sending another wave of anxiety through Emily.

"Stop it, Jack!" Her mother's voice, rarely raised at him, shot back. Then came a frightening cacophony of sounds: shuffling, shoving, and worst of all, her mother's crying. It all ended abruptly with the violent slam of a door, leaving behind only Alexandra's sobs.

The loud thud echoed through the house, jolting Emily back to the harsh reality. Her heart pounded with adrenaline. Even though she tried to barricade herself against the harshness downstairs by closing her eyes tightly, her parents' escalating argument punctured her thin layer of protection.

The vibrations from the raised voices seemed to infiltrate her room through the walls and floor. Every sound—the creaking floorboards, the clink of glass—amplified her fear.

"Just... stop. ... Please... stop," Emily whispered quietly to herself.

The overwhelming smell of her father's alcohol-laden breath seemed to invade every corner, suffocating her with reminders of his volatility. As the shouting continued, a knot of anxiety twisted in Emily's stomach, and a layer of cold sweat formed on her forehead.

"You're useless!" Jack's words cut through the air, his irritation clear in his voice.

"Jack, you're drunk. Just go to bed. We'll talk in the morning," Alexandra tried to defuse the situation.

She drew her knees to her chest instinctively, bracing herself for the temporary silence that usually followed these eruptions.

Each cruel word from downstairs jabbed Emily, her feeling of powerlessness fueling her fear. She wished desperately that she could intervene, to break the cycle, but she knew her presence would only stoke the fire. Instead, she pressed her thumb and forefinger together and focused on distancing her mind from the conflict.

In her secret world, there were no raised voices or looming threats. She found a warm blanket and curled up in the corner. A sense of peace washed over her, dispelling the icy fear that clung to her in the real world. The velvety softness of flower petals under her fingertips, the sweet scent of blooming buds, and the gentle sound of trickling water filled her senses.

The sound of glass shattering downstairs jolted her, her pulse racing with fear. She focused even harder. She believed that if she stayed there, nothing could harm her.

Jack's parents' disappointment cast a long shadow over his life. His father's relentless anger repeatedly assaulted him as a young man.

"I'm not the failure you've made me out to be, Dad. I'm my own person, and I'll prove that to you," Jack would assert.

His father's words would echo in his mind, leaving marks of a worthless fool. Tall and scrawny, Jack shouldered his parents' disapproval, reaching for a love that remained out of grasp, withheld as a punishment for his mere existence.

In a bid for self-worth, Jack would strive to quiet the haunting echoes of his past. Every night, he drowned his father's bitter words in the music at local pool halls, using the sound of billiard balls and laughter as a salve. But this offered only a brief escape from his suffocating insecurity.

A craving for attention always gnawed at him. At gatherings, he made himself the center of attention, narrating animated stories or performing impressive tricks. His actions screamed for visibility, admiration, and celebration. He needed validation from the world.

He treasured each business achievement, each compliment on his taste in clothes or decor, savoring these external approvals. He felt a surge of pride with Alexandra by his side, driven not only by his genuine affection for her but also by his desire to flaunt her elegance.

At every event, he guided her through the crowd, subtly drawing attention to her grace as if saying, 'Look at what I have.' Every approving glance from her endorsed his dreams.

Beneath his flaws, there lived a resilience and fervent longing for redemption. He bore the weight of his past but resolved to rise above it.

His struggles unearthed a strength that contradicted his upbringing and spurred him to alter his story. Jack wanted to prove he was more than his disappointments, that he could construct a life where his dreams coexisted with his flaws. His transformation into a fully realized man resulted from his imperfections, his relentless pursuit of love and acceptance, and his self-discovery, preparing him for future challenges and victories.

Like Jack, Alexandra had to cope with the uncomfortable family dynamics resulting from her mother's incessant need for attention. Every time she engrossed herself in a book or activity, her mother would interrupt, requesting a cup of coffee or conversation, demanding her undivided attention. This made Alexandra feel isolated and frustrated.

Her father, preoccupied with work, was often absent from the family. Despite these challenges, she achieved academic excellence, but her mother expected more than simply good grades. She assigned Alexandra the role of a surrogate parent, thrusting the care of her younger siblings upon her as if they were her own children. This burden was heavy for her young shoulders. The growing weight of her circumstances ignited her desire to escape. Increasingly, she would find herself looking out of her bedroom window, dreaming of her emancipation.

At eighteen, Alexandra leaped at a chance for independence. She took a job as a flight attendant in one of the Midwest's larger cities, craving an opportunity to carve out a life where she could breathe freely. It was there that she met Jack on her journey toward independence. His charismatic charm instantly captivated her.

Watching him stirred a mix of emotions in Alexandra. A warm fluttering in her stomach signaled nervous excitement and burgeoning affection. She admired his looks, his smile, and the intensity of his gaze. She felt herself drawn to him.

His physical appearance, charisma, and vulnerability captivated her. In his arms, she found a sense of security she had never known before. His expansive dreams ignited an intense longing to join him on a voyage toward a world beyond her own limitations.

In Jack, she discovered a soulmate who shared her ambition for a life beyond their past. They embarked on an expedition of dreams and aspirations together, providing each other with support and companionship in their shared loneliness.

She often felt humbled by his presence. His intellectual prowess stirred her admiration. She trusted his wisdom—a wisdom she believed could overcome any challenge. He inspired her. She leaned on his judgment and capabilities to navigate life's complexities. His words and actions reassured her. His confidence's potential stirred deep admiration within her. Although she sometimes felt overshadowed, she comforted herself with the thought that she could contribute to something greater by aligning herself with his vision. Together, they formed a symbiotic bond.

On Saturday mornings, the family gathered for breakfast of bacon, eggs, and toast. Scott and Emily fought over the newspaper comics while their father's voice echoed softly through the house, blending with her mother's laughter, as they engaged in light-hearted conversation.

After breakfast, her father readied himself to leave for a meeting.

"What's the meeting about today, Dad?"

"It's nothing you need to worry about."

Soon after, her mother announced her intention to go shopping.

"Mom, can I come too? I can help with the bags."

"No. I need you to stay here with Scott. He's in charge."

In desperation for a break from the house and from Scott, she begged her mother to let her come with her, but Alexandra firmly declined.

A sense of anxiety gnawed at her as she withdrew to her room, keenly aware of the impending shift in the atmosphere. She knew from experience that the absence of their parent's watchful eyes enabled Scott to turn their home into a battlefield of torment.

In the confines of her bedroom, she would confide in her doll. "Now, Mrs. Beasley, let's just stay in here and play. Maybe he won't notice us."

Bored and seeking amusement, Scott decided to play a prank on Emily, one that he intended to leave an indelible mark. Knowing Emily's vivid imagination and her habit of losing herself in her world, he slipped silently into the garage and picked up a dark, ragged cloak, and a grotesque mask their father had once used for a Halloween costume. He savored his transformation into a frightening figure.

"This is going to be so fun," he muttered to himself.

His heart pounded with anticipation as he crept up to Emily's bedroom door and opened it slowly.

Emily's head snapped up in alarm. As he loomed like a sinister figure in her doorway, her eyes widened in terror. Advancing, the masked brother stretched his arms towards her with his malevolent grin hidden. Emily screamed, scrambling away from him.

"No! Stay back! You're not real! Please don't hurt me!" In a panic, she scurried under her bed, shivering, and sobbing uncontrollably.

Pulling off the mask, he sneered, "Stupid."

He stared down at her peeking out from under the bed, "C'mon, I want you to see something."

Once they were outside, he seized Emily's hand and pulled her along, leading her into the thick woods behind their house.

"See what? Where are we going?"

"You'll see. Just keep moving."

She stumbled over roots and rocks, her heart pounding. The woods, with their deep shadows and rustling undergrowth, had always scared her, but her brother seemed bent on driving her deeper into the trees.

"Can we please go back now? I want to go home," Emily whimpered. Every darkening shadow and every rustle or snap made her jump.

Sensing her fear, her brother scoffed, "You're such an idiot."

Feeling reluctant but without an alternative, she kept following him. The rain and the slippery ground made it hard to keep pace with him. She tripped multiple times, scraping her knees and hands, on the rough ground.

Her brother laughed at her clumsiness. "Can't you walk without falling? You're such a pig."

Emily struggled, trying to match her brother's unyielding pace. She begged him to slow down, but he disregarded her.

"Scott! I can't see anything! Please!" Emily cried. "I can't keep up! Wait for me! Please!"

His cruel smirk haunted her. He halted and whispered in her ear, "You know, one day, you'll get lost in that fantasy world of yours, and no one will save you." Then he darted off, abandoning her in the howling wind and rain. Laughing, he said,

"Good luck finding your way back!"

The thunderstorm raged on, beating Emily with an almost sentient ferocity. The wind lashed her hair around her face, saturating her clothes with rain. Thunder reverberated in her chest, and lightning sporadically illuminated the darkness with an eerie glow.

"Scott! Are you out there?"

In the haunting flashes of light, tears streamed down her cheeks, merging with the raindrops. She sobbed, her voice barely audible above the clamor of the storm. The thought of home invaded her mind, and her tears flowed more freely, each one silently pleading for comfort and safety.

"Please... I just want to go home."

Emily's deep loneliness intensified her fear of the darkness and the storm. She had no one to turn to for help. With each step, she struggled forward, feeling the monumental effort. Fatigue throbbed in her legs, and her body grew numb from the cold.

A deep panic took hold of her. It wasn't the tempest that terrified her, with its thundering roars and punishing winds. The gripping fear of not finding her way back home seized her. The prospect filled her with an ice-cold dread, chillier even than the biting rain.

Growing desperate, she sucked in a deep, shaky breath, wiping away the tears and rain from her cheeks. She embarked on her precarious journey, with each step taking her farther down the path toward home.

To find solace, Emily squeezed her thumb and forefinger together and retreated. In her mind, she envisioned a warm, sunlit meadow filled with colorful wildflowers and gentle butterflies trying to escape the frightful storm. But even there, the darkness and storm loomed, threatening to tear her away.

Her teeth chattered as the wind howled around her, pushing her in every direction, and the trees towered above her like monstrous giants. Fear built up in the pit of her stomach, threatening to consume her completely.

When she finally reached her way home, Emily was exhausted. Soaked and shivering, she pounded on the door. No one answered, and her panic rose.

"Mom! Dad! Please let me in," she shrieked.

She banged harder, calling for her brother, her parents, anyone—but her pleas fell on deaf ears.

"Mama, Daddy, where are you?" Defeated, she sat on the wet porch and wept.

Out of the corner of her eye, she noticed a man. She turned to see the silhouette standing ominously leaning against the corner of the house, watching her. The man was tall, with broad shoulders, dressed in a dark coat that concealed his features. Emily froze, her heart hammering in her chest. He remained silent and still, watching her with cold, unfeeling eyes.

She had seen him before and cried out, "Please stay away from me!"

Using her fists, she pounded on the door again, shouting for her family, but there was still no response.

"Please, somebody help me!" she screamed, her voice desperate. "I'm right here! Please, I'm right here!"

The man continued to watch, his eyes tracking her every movement. Soggy and overwhelmed, she curled up into a ball on the corner of the porch. The rumble of thunder and crackle of lightning sent tremors through her body. She squeezed her eyes shut, pressing her thumb and forefinger together, trying desperately to disappear.

What felt like an eternity passed before Emily finally heard the familiar rumble of her parents' car pulling up to the house. As the car's headlights illuminated the driveway, relief washed over her, and she felt an overwhelming sense of gratitude that they had come to her rescue. Her eyes darted around frantically in search of the man, but he had disappeared into the storm.

As the days passed, Emily couldn't dispel the growing sense of dread that had taken root within her. The man haunted her thoughts, his presence lurking just beyond her line of sight. She increasingly sensed his proximity, the enigmatic stranger in the darkness, always skulking in the periphery.

His unsettling presence served as a perpetual reminder of the dangers surrounding her. The man appeared to be omnipresent — outside her window at night, watching her as she tried to sleep, concealed in the shadows when she walked home from school, standing silently among the trees as she played.

One day, Alexandra and Scott had a particularly awful clash, sparked by an act of cruelty perpetrated by her son and his friends against Jeffrey, the scrawny kid who lived across the street.

Emily saw the whole scene unfold from her spot on the fence line where she was ordered to wait. She was a horrified yet guilt-ridden bystander. Her relief that she wasn't the target of her brother's malicious antics was contaminated with guilt for feeling thankful at Jeffrey's expense. She watched helplessly as they buried him alive, laughing and cheering as they shoveled dirt over his face, with just a drinking straw protruding from the mound for him to breathe through.

The boys reveled in their meanness, taunting the buried boy. "Look at him, what an idiot!" one of them jeered, their amusement only growing with each passing moment.

The scene would have continued unchecked had Maxine, the boy's mother, not come into the backyard.

Upon seeing the freshly dug hole in her lawn, she asked the three boys, "Can you explain to me why you dug up the yard?"

Snickering and pointing fingers led her to the horrifying truth. "Oh, it's just Jeffrey," they said nonchalantly, finding humor in their reckless endangerment of another.

One of them, with a smirk on his face, responded, "Oh, we've just buried Jeff alive. It's hilarious!"

They gestured toward the single straw sticking out of the ground, chuckling, "See? He can breathe just fine!"

They genuinely believed the straw would supply sufficient oxygen for the buried boy, a testament to their dangerous naivety.

Maxine's expression turned from confusion to horror in an instant.

"You did what?! Dig him up. NOW!" she demanded, her voice shaking with fear and fury.

Reluctantly, the boys began digging. Jeffrey was physically unhurt but deeply traumatized, and he darted home in tears. The laughter and jeering ceased, replaced by a deafening silence.

Maxine looked at the three boys, disgusted. She sent her two inside and demanded that Scott go home. The boys scattered, and Scott ran home with Emily close behind.

When they arrived home, Scott grabbed Emily's shirt and pulled her close. "Don't you say a fucking word to Mom or Dad!" Then he threw her to the floor.

As evening descended, Emily, Scott, and Alexandra found themselves together in the kitchen. The aroma of roast beef and mashed potatoes filled the air as Alexandra prepared dinner. Emily's stomach rumbling was a welcome distraction from the day's earlier drama.

The kitchen served as the heart of their home, a hub of constant activity and interaction. Life revolved around this table, transforming it into a witness to their shared joys, disagreements, and the simple, everyday moments that strung their lives together. For a moment, she forgot the day and smiled at her mother.

The piercing ring of the phone suddenly punctuated the tranquility in the kitchen, cutting through the sounds of sizzling food and low chatter. Startled, Alexandra answered the call, her face draining of color as she listened to the quivering voice of Jeffrey's mother on the other end of the line. Sensing the tension, Scott shot a threatening glance at Emily, wordlessly warning her.

When Alexandra hung up, disbelief and anger mixed on her face. She turned to face Scott, her eyes turning cold and hard.

"Scott!" she began, her voice trembling with controlled anger, "Can you explain to me why you thought it was ok to bury Jeffrey alive?"

Silence fell upon the room. Scott's smirk slowly faded as he grasped the severity of her tone.

"It was just a joke, Mom," he replied, trying to shrug it off.

"Just a joke?" Alexandra retorted, her volume rising. "Do you consider burying a boy alive a joke? You could have killed him!"

"But we gave him a straw to breathe through, Mom," he protested.

His defense further fueled his mother's anger. "A straw?!" she exclaimed. "A straw doesn't make it okay, Scott! What if something went wrong? What if he panicked and swallowed the straw?"

Stepping forward, Alexandra imposed her will on him, gritting her teeth. Scott fell silent, his careless demeanor crumbling under the weight of his mother's stare.

"This isn't some harmless prank," Alexandra continued, her voice choked with emotion. "You've gone too far this time. You can't just toy with people's lives for your amusement. We will deal with this when your father gets home. Go to your room."

Silence once again filled the room as Alexandra's heated words lingered in the air. Scott's attempts at justification were replaced by deafening silence. The severity of his actions finally started to sink in, leaving a bitter taste in his mouth. He glared at Emily as he walked by.

Tension mounted in the household. Emily's mother appeared haggard and distant, while her brother's behavior grew increasingly threatening. Recognizing the instability of their moods, she chose to keep her distance and swiftly retreated to her room.

Safe from her brothers anger, Emily flung open her bedroom door, only to be confronted by the eerie sight of the man lurking in the corner, his face shrouded in impenetrable shadows. A chilling wave of terror washed over her, paralyzing her in place. The air turned stagnant, thick with an unsettling stillness that amplified her fear.

He took a step closer and leaned in, whispering to her, "Be careful, girl." His voice was low and enigmatic, sending a shiver down her spine. "There are things hidden in the shadows, waiting and watching," he said, his tone laced with an underlying menace. "I am always nearby, even when you least expect it. You are never alone."

The man's words lingered in the air, leaving Emily unsettled. "If you need me... well... just say so," he added, his voice taking on an almost deceptive kindness.

Panic surged through her. She shut her eyes, desperately trying to vanish, but the man's whispers intensified, drowning her thoughts.

"They will deceive you," he breathed, his voice almost seductive.

His words struck a nerve, fueling her unease and causing her to question the trust she had placed in those around her. Silent screams stuck in her throat as she pressed her thumb and forefinger together, desperately seeking solace. When she opened her eyes, she found the room empty, as if the man had dissolved into the very shadows that once shrouded him.

Emily blinked in disbelief, searching every corner, but there was no trace of him. An eerie silence hung in the air, leaving her bewildered. Trembling, she crawled into bed, tears streaming down her face, her heart heavy with unanswered questions and fear.

Immersed in the pages of a novel, Emily huddled under the covers, allowing the story to transport her to another world. The soft blanket against her skin brought a comforting warmth, enveloping her in a private shelter of her imagination. In the background, the soothing rhythm of the vacuum resonated through the house, its low hum blending with the sound of the clothes dryer. The faint scent of clean carpets and freshly washed laundry mingled with the pages of her book enveloped Emily in a shroud of literature and domestic peacefulness.

"Emily, honey, could you get the phone if it rings?" Alexandra's voice floated up from downstairs. "I don't want to stop halfway."

Before she could respond, the calm was shattered as the front door abruptly slammed. The startling percussion gave way to an unexpected sound—a burst of joyful laughter that rumbled from deep in her father's chest. The laughter filled the house, as Jack exuded effervescence, buoyant on the success of his newly established construction company. A success that had transformed their typically quiet house into a carnival of joy.

"Alexandra, we did it! We've finally got our big break!" His hearty voice resonated through the walls.

Her mother's giggles harmonized with his excitement, creating a happy melody rarely heard under that roof.

"You've earned this. We've earned this!" she chimed in, her voice vivacious and cheerful. "Emily, Scott, come down here. Let's all celebrate together."

An unfamiliar jollity coursed through the veins of the house, pulsing through the halls, up the stairs, and into Emily's room.

Confused, Emily could feel her lips curling up in a hesitant smile. A part of her wanted to join the festivities, to allow herself to be swept up in the whirlwind. But she paused at the banister, taking in the scene below, feeling anticipation curling in her stomach.

Her father bounded up the stairs, cutting through the riotous cheer. This time, his voice was softer, more fatherly.

"Come downstairs, Emily. We're celebrating."

"Okay, Daddy."

Taking his hand, she descended the stairs, her tentative steps growing more confident as she neared the living room.

Her father let out a whoop, his booming voice echoing in the room.

"There's our little princess," he declared, swinging Emily around in a dizzying spin.

Laughter bubbled from her as she clung to him.

As they spun and swayed to the rhythm of the music, she couldn't help but be happy. This was a rare moment of unbridled joy. For the first time in a long time, Emily felt a glimmer of excitement, a moment of spontaneous bliss was a welcome reprieve.

Emily hated Sunday. Her father and mother rarely attended Mass with their children. Her father wanted to relax—it was his day off, after all—and he wasn't interested in Mass. Her mother, a devout Catholic, struggled between caring for her husband and ensuring her children learned the Catechism. So, each Sunday, she got them properly dressed and sent them on the long walk to church. The journey to Mass became a tormenting obstacle course as Scott took perverse delight in hurling rocks at her and baiting her with relentless jibes.

"Scott, please, stop it. It's Sunday. Can't you just be nice to me for once?" Emily pleaded, trying to quell her brother's aggression.

Arriving at the church, they discreetly settled themselves in the back pew, their eyes flickering towards the exit as they bid their time, anticipating the opportune moment to slip away.

As the congregation prepared for communion, he would subtly cue her with a whisper, "Let's go."

With a nod of understanding, she would fall into step behind him, silently slipping out into the freedom beyond the church's doors.

Each week, a ritual unfolded with alarming regularity. Emily's hands shook, weighed down by guilt, as she stealthily pilfered money from the poor box under her brother's watchful gaze. Scott assigned himself the role of lookout, standing alert and scanning the room for approaching parishioners.

"Hurry up, Emily! Grab it and let's get out of here," Scott yanked her arm impatiently, his eyes darting nervously around the sacred room. As soon as she had the money, Scott would pocket it without a hint of remorse, his eyes cold and unflinching.

Their return from church became a race, as the tranquil surroundings were punctuated by the thundering footfalls of the siblings. The sight of their house from the road triggered an uncontrollable reaction in Emily. Urine trickled down her leg, the warm sensation conflicting with the icy fear gripping her heart.

"Not again, Emily! How can you be so... well... you?" said Scott, disgust palpable in his voice.

Scott's reaction was predictably unpredictable. His barrage of insults was punctuated with sharp punches to her back.

"I told you to stop that! You're disgusting!" He spat the words out, his voice filled with a venomous rage that terrified Emily.

He left her standing there to find her own way home.

As she topped the crest of the hill, her eyes caught the disconcerting sight of the familiar man. He was oddly perched in a tree, his piercing gaze fixed firmly on her. A cold shiver raced down her spine, tightening her chest with fear. The only route home lay dangerously close to him, turning the familiar path into a foreboding gauntlet.

For several heart-thudding minutes, she stood paralyzed on the spot, her gaze locked with his, silently pleading with him to abandon his unsettling vigil. But he remained unmoved, a silent scout, watching and waiting, like a spider at the center of its web.

Finally, summoning a surge of desperate courage, she took a shaky breath and broke into a frantic run. Her foot caught on a hidden root, and she found herself tumbling down the slope, the world spinning around her in a disorienting whirl. She landed with a jarring thud that knocked the breath from her lungs.

Wincing, she pushed herself up and began to sprint once more, her heart pounding in her chest like a desperate drum.

As she raced past him, her senses heightened. She could almost feel his gaze, a physical weight on her back. A chilling laugh echoed in her ears, a disturbing accompaniment to her flight. It was soft, almost whispering, yet it resonated in the quiet air, enhancing her fear and propelling her faster toward the safety of her home.

At home, her mother greeted her with an exasperated rebuke. "Emily! How many times do I have to tell you? This can't happen every week!"

Roughly cleaning her up, her mother's voice rang out, sharp and accusing, "What's wrong with you?" The question hung in the air, a bitter reminder of the twisted reality of Emily's Sunday rituals.

Emily had no answers. Confusion clouded her young mind, as the labels "stupid" and "broken" carved themselves into her consciousness. She felt a profound sense of brokenness, caught in a conundrum that defied her comprehension—a puzzle piece that didn't fit, no matter how much she tried. Her heart carried a silent question, an echo resounding in the quiet corners of her existence— Why? Why was she this way?

Emily discovered a hidden retreat on a day when Scott was in an especially sour mood. He spitefully ordered her to eat a serving of hardened, three-day-old oatmeal at the breakfast table. She refused, and he towered over her, ruthlessly smacking the back of her head.

He taunted, "Eat it," slapping her again. "Come on, just eat it." Another slap.

Tears pricked at her eyes, but she stood her ground. The standoff lasted more than an hour, only ending when a phone call diverted Scott's attention. This was her chance. She tore away from the dining room, seeking solace in the depths of her closet.

Scrambling onto the topmost shelf, she buried herself under heaps of blankets and cushions, her ears alert to Scott's shouts that reverberated through the house.

"Emily, I'll find you, and when I do..." His promise was an ominous storm cloud, intensifying her resolve to stay out of sight.

She lay silently on her back. Looking up, her eyes locked onto a small, unnoticed hatch in the ceiling.

As his voice grew louder and nearer, she placed her feet on the hatch and quietly counted to herself, "One, two, three, and push..."

To her shock and delight, the hatch gave way, unveiling a mysterious, unexplored area.

Her heart raced as she climbed inside, whispering to herself, "Please, let this work." She carefully slid the panel back into place, cloaking herself, hoping her brother wouldn't notice her hiding spot. It worked.

Enveloped in protective darkness, she listened to the erratic thumping of her heart slowly return to a steady rhythm. A heavy, profound silence hung in the air, lulling her senses. Then, like a breeze blowing through a forest, the front door opened, and the familiar, soothing timbre of her parents' voices filled the void.

Alexandra called, "Kids, we're home," the words bringing instant relief. Emily's rigid body relaxed. With trembling hands, she tentatively nudged the concealed panel open, allowing a thin beam of soft light to pierce the darkness.

Taking a deep, cleansing breath, she gingerly stepped down from her high perch in the closet. She swiftly but carefully closed the hatch, ensuring the secrecy of her newfound sanctum. Her bare feet hit the cold, wooden floor of her bedroom with a light thud, and she slid down to sit, drawing her knees up to her chest. A flicker of adventurous spirit danced in her eyes, silently promising the stories yet to unfold within the walls of her hidden haven.

In the kitchen, Emily's mother turned, a surprised smile lighting up her face. "Emily, there you are! How was your day?" Her voice was warm.

Emily mustered a smile. "Oh, you know, just the usual. It was fine, Mom. How about yours?"

Her mother's eyes narrowed slightly, sensing something beneath Emily's composed facade.

"Are you sure everything's all right, sweetheart? You seem a bit... odd."

"I'm fine." Her voice quivered slightly, but she kept her composure. Casually glancing at her brother, she added, "Nothing out of the ordinary."

Over the next few months, Emily dedicated herself to the transformation of her covert sanctuary hidden in the attic's secluded rafters.

In her moments of solitude, the muffled padding of her footsteps echoed gently, disrupting the still silence as she carried her possessions into this secret space. Each item, once introduced into the attic with its dimly lit, weather-worn wood and sharp-edged shadows, was like a new member joining a clandestine society.

Emily furnished her personal niche within the attic, tucked under the sharply sloping roof. She curated a collection of small treasures: fragments of colored glass that shimmered as they caught slivers of sunlight filtering through the small hatch, pebbles worn smooth by time and etched with intricate patterns, and oddly shaped twigs that felt rough under her fingertips. Every item, when set on the wooden floor, produced a soft scratching sound.

The attic remained quiet, punctuated only by the occasional distant cooing of pigeons nesting in the external eaves and the soft whistle of the wind threading through the narrow gaps in the timeworn wood. The hushed rustling of her dolls' clothing and the gentle thud of their button eyes and stitched smiles against the wooden floor added a playful liveliness to the static space.

The attic, steeped in a nostalgic blend of the old house's aroma, the subtle scent of her dolls' fabric, and the earthy fragrance of the twigs, evolved into a personal theater. Bathed in subdued light, Emily and her dolls would spend hours spinning enthralling tales.

Emily's hideaway wasn't entirely isolated from the outside world. Now and then, the stillness would be disrupted by Scott's thunderous voice. "Emily!" he cried out, clearly agitated.

His escalating annoyance rippled through the wooden floorboards and bounced off the high ceilings.

"Emily, where the hell are you?" Scott demanded, exasperated.

Each time his frustrated voice echoed through her hideaway, she felt an unexpected thrill.

"Emily! Get your ass out here NOW!"

He intended to instill fear, but instead, he fueled her sense of triumph. She giggled, realizing she was completely undetectable.

"She must be here somewhere," he muttered to himself, oblivious to her sly smile.

She had become a needle expertly concealed in a haystack. But her tranquility was short-lived.

Emily was deeply immersed in her imaginary world, weaving tales with her dolls, when she was jolted back to reality. The hatch that guarded her private world slid open abruptly, causing her heart to skip. An intrusive arm, strong and uninvited, reached in and grabbed onto her dress.

Her father's features contorted in an expression of rage she had never seen. The sight left her momentarily breathless.

"Emily, what the hell is wrong with you? This attic is off-limits. I don't want you playing up here, understand?"

Each syllable was hard and cold like shards of ice jabbed into her ears. His tone was unyielding, leaving no room for negotiation.

"Yes, sir." Her voice was small and compliant.

The following day, she watched as her father hammered nail after nail into the hatch. Each ringing clash was a bitter reminder of her loss, her secret hideaway now an inaccessible dream.

As Scott stood back and watched, a cruel and triumphant smirk played on his lips. He basked in her sadness.

"You're an idiot, Emily," he jeered, his voice laced with amusement.

With a last forceful blow of the hammer, the entrance to her cherished hiding place was sealed shut. She stared at the hatch, her eyes misty with unshed tears.

Emily had become accustomed to her mother's fragile moods and consciously mirrored her demeanor. Most days, her mother's gentle words embraced her like a soft touch, while the subtle scent of her presence offered familiar comfort. However, birthday celebrations and other events that most children took for granted were absent from her experience. Her mother believed such celebrations spoiled a child.

So, when Alexandra suddenly announced that she would host a birthday party for Emily, a whirlwind of emotions swept through her. It felt as if an unexpected summer storm had engulfed her, exciting sensations tingling through her fingertips, disbelief echoing in her ears, and a touch of apprehension fluttering in her chest. The idea of a birthday party, ordinary for others, took on an extraordinary and surreal quality, like the delicate fragrance of a dream.

The park, their town's secret heart, and Emily's refuge from the noise of life served as the backdrop for her introduction to the chaotic world of social gatherings. As they prepared for the party, a symphony of sensory delights unfolded. The kitchen transformed into a lively hub of culinary activity, filled with laughter and clattering utensils, permeated by tantalizing aromas.

The comforting scent of a freshly baked cake wafted through the room, beckoning with its warm, sweet embrace. The crisp crunch of slicing fresh bread mingled with the rhythmic melody of sandwich-making, creating a vibrant ambiance. Vibrant streamers and balloons adorned the scene, splashing colors across the space.

"Emily, could you hand me those balloons?" Alexandra asked, her voice soft yet brimming with excitement, as she busily prepared the sandwiches. Emily's fingers brushed against the smooth surface of the balloons, their buoyancy dancing beneath her touch as she passed them to her mother.

On the day of the party, the sun made its grand entrance, casting a golden glow upon the park. The radiant warmth enveloped Emily, infusing her with a sense of vitality and anticipation. With each arrival of Emily's classmates, their smiling faces illuminated her world, and their laughter filled the air.

"Happy birthday, Emily!"

"Wow, this looks amazing! Your mom did an impressive job!"

"Emily, your party is going to be the best one ever!"

She reveled in the mingling scents of freshly cut grass and blooming flowers, nature's fragrant offering to the celebration. The taste of anticipation lingered on her tongue, blending sweet excitement and tangy anticipation. The party unfolded like a vibrant tableau, engaging all the senses. Laughter resounded in the air, buoyant and contagious, weaving its way into Emily's heart. Friendly hands brushed against hers during games, sending ripples of connection through her fingertips, and the delectable flavors of party treats exploded on her palate, creating a symphony of taste sensations. Conversations intertwined in a tapestry of voices, rising and falling like a melodic chorus.

They sang, "Happy birthday, Emily!" Their voices blended into a chorus of warmth and joy, reverberating within her, wrapping her in a cocoon of celebration. She looked up from the cake, smiling and saw the man leaning on a tree, watching. Their eyes connected and he nodded as if to acknowledge her celebration. She shuddered and blew out her candles, pretending she did not see him.

Even as the evening descended, the party's resonance lingered within Emily. Her lips remained curved into a smile that seemed to have taken up permanent residence, visually reflecting her inner joy. Her heart had found a new rhythm, propelling her from a quiet bystander to an active participant in her own life, its beat pulsating with the vibrant memories etched in her mind.

That night Emily lay wide awake in her bed, her senses attuned to the stillness of the night. The silence shattered as the window creaked open, a haunting sound that jolted her from her thoughts.

Her heart raced within her chest, threatened by the terror that constricted her breath. Paralyzed by fear, she fought to stifle any sound that might invite further danger, her mouth clamped shut. Helpless and motionless, she lay frozen in her bed.

The dim light seeped through the thin curtains, casting an eerie frame around the intruder who entered her room. His silhouette loomed, its undefined contours stretching long shadows across the sparsely furnished space. He embodied a ghostly presence, yet his existence was tangible and rooted in silence. His eyes fixed on her with unsettling patience.

Outwardly, Emily appeared serene, her body still beneath the covers, mimicking the rhythm of deep slumber. Her closed eyes concealed the tempest raging within her. A storm of thoughts and emotions clashed violently, swirling like untamed beasts. Breathing became a struggle, as each inhalation fought against suffocating silence.

The air in the room thickened, pressing against her skin, suffocating her. The soft glow of the nightlight enveloped her in a surreal haze, creating an atmosphere of palpable tension between Emily and the silent watcher. The silence itself became an oppressive force, bearing down on her with crushing weight.

With eerie precision, he peeled back the layers of her bedding, exposing her delicate form to the cool night air. The fabric protested softly as it unfolded, heightening her repulsion. The sensation was bitter, as if she had swallowed something foul, twisting her insides and intensifying her heartbeat.

He eased himself onto the edge of the bed with deliberate slowness, causing the mattress to emit a soft creak. She sensed his proximity, feeling the clash between the warmth of his body and the coolness of the room. His large, imposing hand grazed her shoulder, leaving her nerves screaming in protest. His fingers trailed through her hair, their touch a chilling blend of familiarity and unfamiliarity. It was a paradox that deepened her horror.

To amplify the disturbing scene, he began to hum quietly, a disconcerting melody that invaded her ears. Summoning her dwindling strength, Emily forced her lips to move, her voice raw and strained. "Please... please leave me alone." Each word scraped against her throat like shards of glass, draining her resolve.

"Shh... Don't be scared. Happy Birthday." he whispered from the foot of her bed, his sinister words slithering up her spine. Tears welled in Emily's eyes, threatening to spill over as she found the courage to speak once more. Her voice trembled as she uttered, "I don't want you here." Her final word pierced the silence, sending ripples through the figure at the foot of her bed.

"I am not going to hurt you. Now be quiet," he responded, his tone colder, ice against her heated body. "I promise, you don't want to wake anyone." Ignoring her tears, he continued his twisted serenade, his fingers still caressing her hair with a deceptive tenderness.

Trapped in overwhelming fear, Emily's world spun, her vision narrowing to a blur of shapes and colors. The man's haunting humming lingered in her ears as darkness claimed her, swallowing her consciousness.

The next day, Emily awoke, finding herself snugly tucked into bed. Confusion washed over her, and doubts crept in, questioning whether it had all been a dream. Despite feeling sore and weary, she mustered the strength to gather herself, get dressed, and walk to school.

Seated on the hard surface of her small wooden desk, she struggled to focus on the day's lesson. The teacher's voice served as a comforting background drone as she meticulously guided the class through the complexities of multiplication tables, explaining the steps with patience and precision. The teacher emphasized the importance of mastering the foundational building blocks for more complex math problems, particularly highlighting the significance of the six times table.

Emily's thoughts wandered, torn between her concealed world and the man who tormented her. Absentmindedly gazing at her textbook, she suddenly felt a chill run down her spine. Her heart skipped a beat, and a sense of unease gripped her. Lifting her eyes from her book, she scanned the room, searching for the source of her discomfort.

Horror washed over her as her eyes widened, fixated on the window across the classroom. There, amidst the sunlit playground and the laughter of her classmates, stood the man. He peered at her from behind the glass, his face obscured by shadows, creating a stark contrast to the cheerful scene outside.

Fear consumed her as tears welled up in her eyes. She couldn't tear her gaze away from the man, her body trembling with anxiety. Every instinct urged her to escape his stare, but she knew she couldn't without drawing attention to herself and the man who haunted her. Conflicted, she grappled with whether to seek help or keep the man's existence a secret to shield herself from potential ridicule.

Amidst sobs, she found her voice and cried out, "Miss Johnson! There's a man... outside... and he's watching me!" Panic filled her voice, capturing her teacher's attention.

Alarmed, the teacher rushed to Emily's side, perplexed by the sudden outburst. Through tears, Emily tried to explain what she had seen, gesturing towards the window and the man who had been watching her.

When the teacher and classmates turned to look, however, they found nothing but an empty playground. The teacher furrowed her brow, a mix of concern and disbelief crossing her face as she tried to understand Emily's distress alongside the peaceful scene outside.

In an attempt to console her, the teacher responded, "Emily, dear, there's no one there. Are you sure you're okay? Would you like to see the nurse?"

Her voice carried a soothing tone, aiming to calm the distressed girl. The man had vanished, leaving no trace of his presence. Emily's heart sank as she realized that no one would believe her, and the burden of the man's secret would rest solely on her shoulders.

Emily thought to herself, "I can't tell anyone. They'll think I'm crazy."

As the teacher tried to offer comfort, Emily felt more isolated than ever. Her classmates whispered and exchanged skeptical glances, their curiosity mingled with doubt.

A student from across the room chimed in, saying, "Did any of you see anyone? I didn't see anyone. Emily's just making things up."

As Emily walked home from school, her steps measured and unhurried, her heart weighed heavily in her chest. She dreaded the conversation she knew she had to have with her parents.

Worries consumed her, fearing they might dismiss her experiences or not grasp the gravity of the situation. The incident in class had made it clear—she could no longer keep the man's presence a secret. She needed her parents' help, understanding, and protection.

At home, Emily found her mother in the kitchen, preparing dinner, while her father relaxed in his favorite armchair, reading the newspaper. Taking a deep breath, she approached them tentatively.

"Mom, Dad, there's something I need to talk to you about. It's important," Emily said, her eyes darting nervously between her parents.

She clutched her shirt, trying to steady herself. "It's about... the man I told you about before."

Her voice barely audible, she began recounting her encounters with the man.

She told them about the first time she had seen him and how he had appeared at school that day. Emily's voice trembled with emotion as she explained her hidden world and her efforts to elude the man's grasp.

Tears welled up in her eyes as she pleaded with her parents to believe her. "This isn't a fairy tale. This is real. It's happening. Why don't you believe me? I don't know what to do. I'm scared."

Emily's parents exchanged apprehensive glances as they processed their daughter's words. Uncertain about how to interpret the story, they were torn between concern for her well-being and the unsettling thought that she might be fabricating it all for attention.

Her father exhaled, setting aside his newspaper as he searched for the right words to respond.

"Emily, we love you and want to help you, but this is difficult for us to understand." Worry etched his face.

"You don't understand—he's everywhere!" Emily exclaimed.

He explained to her that while they deeply cared for her, they struggled to accept the man's existence. They suggested that her vivid imagination was playing tricks on her and that her hidden worlds were a manifestation of her desire to escape the challenges in her life.

Her mother gently patted her hand. "Maybe it would be helpful to talk to someone, like a counselor, who could help you sort things out."

Emily looked at her parents in disbelief. "But I'm telling the truth. Can't you see that?"

Emily's heart shattered as she realized that her parents didn't believe her. They thought she was inventing stories to seek attention. Tears streamed down her cheeks as she insisted that the man was real.

"I'm not making this up! Why won't you believe me?"

She felt deeply disappointed and betrayed, knowing that her parents weren't taking her concerns seriously.

Irritated, her father sent her to her room.

"Emily, enough! Go to your room and calm down. We'll discuss this later when everyone is more level-headed."

Tears continued to flow down her face. "I'm not crazy! I don't need to calm down! I need you to listen!"

As Emily lay in bed that night, she felt more isolated than ever. Her parents' skepticism weighed heavily on her, intensifying the burden of the man's presence. Sleep eluded her as she realized she couldn't rely on her parents for protection. Even her imaginary world seemed less comforting than before. In the darkness, Emily whispered to herself, "No one believes me... I'm alone."

The days passed and Emily grew increasingly detached from herself. It was a strange and unsettling sensation, as if she were merely an observer of her own life. The girl she saw in the mirror each morning felt like a stranger, a hollow reflection. She felt like a marionette, going through the motions of daily life while watching from a distance.

Unexpectedly, Emily developed an unusual habit that anchored her to reality. Throughout the day, unnoticed by others, she would slip away from her classroom and seek solace in the quiet of the school bathroom. In those stolen moments, she tightly gripped a pencil in her hand and pressed the hard graphite tip against her thigh, puncturing her skin.

Each prick served as a tangible reminder of her physical self.

It became a strangely soothing ritual, a way to reconnect with her body. The pain brought a fleeting sense of connection, a respite from the numbness that consumed her existence. It was a desperate attempt to feel something, anything, amidst the overwhelming emptiness. But the pain also amplified her misery. Each mark on her thigh was a visible manifestation of her despair. Emily sank deeper into a dark abyss, desperately searching for a way out.

One day, as she hurriedly left the classroom, her teacher halted her exit, their eyes meeting in an uncomfortable confrontation. A flush of embarrassment spread across Emily's face as her classmates stared at her, intensifying her vulnerability. Tears welled up, threatening to spill down her cheeks, betraying her inner turmoil.

Desperate to escape their judgmental gazes, Emily dashed out of the classroom, seeking refuge in a bathroom stall. Her footsteps echoed through the empty hallway as she retreated into the small, confined space, yearning for a moment of respite. With trembling hands, she locked the stall door, isolating herself from the outside world.

Her teacher, filled with concern, followed her into the bathroom, their footsteps echoing urgently.

Peering through the narrow gaps between the stall doors, the teacher caught a glimpse of Emily's tear-streaked face.

"What's wrong, Emily? Can you tell me?" Her voice was soft, brimming with empathy.

But lost in the chaos of her thoughts and emotions, Emily couldn't articulate her distress. Her words escaped her, swallowed by the overwhelming turmoil within.

When Emily remained silent, the teacher's patience waned.

"Emily, you must come out of the bathroom and return to class immediately," she demanded.

Reluctantly, Emily unlocked the stall door and appeared. Every step she took toward the classroom felt heavy, burdened by the judgment she knew awaited her.

As she reentered the classroom, laughter erupted from her classmates. Their innocent cruelty pierced her fragile composure. She tried to shield herself from the mockery, but tears welled up in her eyes.

Trembling, she prayed, "Please... just stop."

The laughter drowned out her words, deepening her sense of isolation. The classroom had become hostile territory, a constant reminder of her differences, vulnerability, and the ease with which she could be targeted.

Emily's father immersed himself in carefully curating his interests and indulging in various pursuits, with aviation being his favorite. As he tirelessly developed his personal brand, he found freedom in the cockpit of a small plane. Getting his pilot's license became a source of immense delight, as he savored the solitary hours spent airborne, navigating the open skies. His ability in flying not only brought personal triumph but also captivated his clients, fostering strong connections in his business endeavors.

Shortly after Emily's episode at school, in an uncharacteristic moment, Jack surprised Emily by declaring, "You and I are going to Chicago."

Excitement surged within her as she eagerly embraced the opportunity to go with him. The prospect of exploring the bustling streets, iconic landmarks, and vibrant energy of Chicago filled her with anticipation. Boarding the plane with her father, her mind buzzed with vivid visions of their impending adventure.

The plane accelerated down the runway, unleashing a surge of adrenaline within Emily as it gracefully lifted off the ground. The powerful rumble of the engines reverberated through her body, harmonizing with her heightened emotions. Emily's eyes remained fixated on the passing scenery, searching for familiarity among the blur of colors and shapes that gradually transformed the landscape.

Leaning closer to the window, her father pointed and said,

"Look, Emily. That's our house right down there." Following his finger, Emily's heart skipped a beat as she discovered the tiny speck on the ground, barely discernible amidst the sprawling houses and streets.

Delight and nostalgia coursed through her, and she couldn't help but exclaim, "I see it!" Excitement filled her voice, infused with the joy of recognition.

With a smile and animated eyes, Jack affirmed, "Yes, that's our home. We'll be back before you know it."

However, as the plane ascended higher, the distinct features of their house merged into the tapestry of the city below. Mixed with the exhilaration of the unknown, a hint of anxiety fluttered within Emily as she left the comfort of her familiar surroundings.

Yet, it was her father's unexpected gesture that kindled an extraordinary level of excitement.

Jack, typically reserved, turned to her with a gleam in his eyes and said, "Hold on to the controls. Feel the plane."

The resonating words sparked a surge of anticipation within her, and she eagerly reached out, grasping the cool metal of the control column.

Filled with awe and disbelief, Emily asked, "Really, Dad? Can I do it?" Her voice quivered with a mixture of emotions, her eyes shining with wonder.

Nodding, Jack affirmed, "Absolutely, Emily. I trust you. Just follow my lead and enjoy yourself."

The cabin reverberated with the symphony of sounds—the hum of the engines, the whistling of the wind, and the occasional radio chatter from the cockpit. The unique aroma of aviation fuel mingled with the sterile cabin scent, immersing them in a captivating backdrop as their adventure unfolded.

As they soared through the sky, Emily's senses heightened. The panoramic view outside the windows painted a tapestry of breathtaking beauty— fluffy white clouds stretched as far as the eye could see, while the earth below resembled a patchwork quilt of vibrant greens and earthy browns.

"Look, Dad! It's like we're floating above the world," she remarked, her voice filled with awe, capturing the profound sense of wonderment.

Acknowledging her observation, Jack nodded, "Flying gives us a whole new perspective, doesn't it? It's a feeling of freedom and limitless possibilities."

In that unforgettable moment, Emily assumed the role of a co-pilot under her father's watchful eye. The shared joy and exhilaration enveloped them, transcending the confines of the metal and machinery surrounding them. Together, they forged a bond that would forever be etched in their memories.

Overwhelmed by the incredible experience, Emily exclaimed, "I can't believe we're doing this, Dad."

With unwavering enthusiasm, Jack responded, "You're my co-pilot, Emily. Today, we navigate the skies together."

When they reached Chicago, Emily's father wasted no time arranging for a car.

"We need transportation," he said, prompting the swift acquisition of a vehicle.

They drove through the city's bustling arteries in an uncomfortable silence that matched the energetic ambiance outside. Eventually, they pulled over on a lively street along the banks of the Hudson River. A charming, family-run curio shop that also served sodas and milkshakes awaited them.

Stepping into the shop, Emily's father withdrew a crisp twenty-dollar bill and handed it to the lady behind the counter. He issued his instructions with a tone of authority,

"Keep a watchful eye on my daughter while I'm gone." His words were brief and resolute.

He turned to Emily, his gaze stern, and asked, "Stay put and don't leave the shop. Do you understand me?"

"Yes, sir," Emily replied, her voice tinged with uncertainty.

Without further explanation, he exited the shop, leaving Emily alone with a total stranger. Aware of the consequences of defying her father, Emily obediently stood still, her apprehension mingling with fear.

The woman at the counter became a source of comfort for Emily. Warmth radiated from her, and her welcoming smile pierced through Emily's unease like a lighthouse cutting through the fog. The lady's amiability was a stark contrast to her father's distant demeanor, which had left Emily feeling adrift.

Donning a vintage apron adorned with floral patterns reminiscent of a cozy home kitchen, the lady's eyes sparkled with genuine interest. Her laughter echoed amidst the array of antique trinkets and bottles of soda. Each time their eyes met, she offered a small nod or a reassuring smile, gestures that spoke volumes about her kindness.

Amid her various tasks, such as serving customers, dusting off shelves, and arranging oddities in the display window, the shopkeeper never let Emily stray too far from her attention. Occasionally, she paused to engage Emily in light conversation or to share intriguing anecdotes about the items in the shop.

"Look at this little porcelain doll here. It's from the late nineteenth century. Doesn't she bear a striking resemblance to you?" the woman chuckled, inviting Emily's opinion.

Emily shrugged, her thoughts consumed by her father's absence.

As the hours ticked by and the sun began its descent below the horizon, the shop filled with a golden hue as the fading light filtered through the vintage windows. Emily's initial fear had evolved into a gnawing pit in her stomach. The hands of the antique clock on the wall seemed to mock her with each passing moment.

Doubts clouded Emily's mind, obscuring her positive thoughts. The nagging thought that her father might not return grew stronger as twilight cast its warm glow upon the shop's interior, intensifying Emily's anxiety.

Gripping the edge of her chair with apprehension, she whispered, "What if he doesn't come back?"

Just as despair threatened to consume her, her father reentered the shop. His face betrayed no emotion as he motioned for Emily to follow him. "We're leaving."

They quickly returned to the local airport, silence enveloped father and daughter, hanging heavy in the air. The scent of jet fuel lingered, intermingling with the cool, metallic tang of the aircraft's interior. The plane sat poised on the runway, its metallic skin gleaming under the floodlights, and its solitary propeller spinning in anticipation.

Methodically, Emily's father prepared for their flight. The clicking sound of switches being flipped and buttons being pressed filled the cabin, accompanied by the faint hum of the engine. He checked dials, their smooth surfaces cool to the touch, secured seat belts with a satisfying click, and got the plane ready for takeoff. Each action was executed with precision, the oppressive silence amplifying the significance of every movement. From her seat, Emily saw her father's actions with a mix of fascination and detachment. She was captivated by his confidence and ease in using the plane's complex controls.

"Fasten your seat belt," her father instructed, breaking the silence. The distinctive sound of the seat belt latch clicking into place echoed through the cabin. "We're about to take off."

They ascended into the fading dusk, the plane humming with mechanical vitality. The rush of wind against the fuselage created a symphony of sound, blending with the soft vibrations that coursed through the cabin. Emily's gaze shifted between the receding cityscape below, the glimmering lights of Chicago transforming into a distant starry pattern.

Inside the confined cabin, every sound reverberated. The soft creak of leather seats as they shifted, the gentle clicks of adjusting dials, and the sporadic crackle of the communication radio created a symphony of mechanical sounds that accompanied their ride home. The peculiar comfort found within the daunting quiet.

Throughout the flight, Emily's father kept his silence, his focus devoted to piloting the plane. The cabin lights cast long, muted shadows across his face, masking his expressions and leaving Emily adrift amidst unanswered questions. Uncertainty swirled in her mind as she stared into the vast expanse of the night sky, the soft glow from the instrument panel supplying a subtle illumination.

The weight of her father's silence bore heavily upon Emily, casting a palpable sense of unease within her. The absence of his words created a void, a chasm of unspoken emotions that stretched between them. It was a silence that carried an unspoken tension, leaving Emily yearning for connection and understanding.

As they sat together in the plane, the silence grew thicker with each passing moment. Emily couldn't help but question herself, wondering what she had done to deserve such silence from her father. His quiet felt like a wall, separating them, and stifling any chance for open communication. It left her feeling isolated and adrift, as if her thoughts and concerns had no place in their shared world.

The lack of words also made Emily question her own worth, fueling a storm of self-doubt. Did her father's silence imply disappointment or disapproval? Did it reflect a lack of interest in her or an inability to connect? These thoughts swirled in her mind, weaving a complex web of insecurities that threatened to overshadow her sense of self.

Emily longed for her father to break the silence, to reach out and bridge the emotional gap that had formed between them. She yearned for him to share his thoughts, fears, and hopes, and to let her do the same. But his steadfast silence only deepened the rift, leaving her feeling unheard and unseen.

In the confines of the aircraft, the silence amplified the weight of their unspoken words. Every passing minute magnified the unanswered questions and unexpressed emotions, further isolating Emily in her thoughts. The silence became a haunting presence, a constant reminder of the unspoken tensions and unresolved issues that lingered between them.

As they finally landed, the small plane gracefully glided down the runway before coming to a rest. Ground crew members bustled around them, their movements accompanied by the distant rumble of engines and the sharp sound of footsteps on the tarmac.

As they drove home, the familiar glow of city lights flickered past, casting fleeting glimpses into their surroundings. The comforting warmth of the car's heater enveloped Emily, contrasting with the cool night air outside. However, Jack's silence persisted, permeating their interactions. It created an invisible barrier, making it difficult for Emily to engage with her father on an emotional level. The lack of communication left her feeling disconnected and estranged.

When the car pulled into their driveway, the old brick mansion loomed before them, bathed in the soft light of the starlit sky. Home offered little solace to Emily; it felt unfamiliar, like a stranger.

Without uttering a word, Emily stepped out of the car, hugging her jacket tightly against the night's chill. She pushed open the front door and ascended the staircase that led to her room. The sound of her footsteps echoed through the eerily silent house, the faint creaking of the wooden steps adding to the atmosphere of solitude.

Reaching the top of the stairs, her mother greeted them with a smile. However, upon catching sight of Jack's expression, she swiftly guided Emily towards her bedroom, her voice filled with concern.

"Come, Emily, let's get you to bed," her mother said, her tone soft and soothing.

Emily complied, her footsteps light as she followed her mother's lead. The bed's familiar coolness enveloped her as she settled into its comforting embrace. The weight of the day's events lingered, casting a heavy burden upon her heart. Closing her eyes, she yearned for a sense of clarity that had remained elusive.

In the encompassing darkness, occasional sounds from passing cars wafted in through the window, punctuating the stillness with fleeting reminders of the outside world. The muffled voices of her parents conversing in the kitchen reached her ears, their words barely audible. Emily's mind churned with restlessness as she lay in silence, straining to decipher their conversation. Unanswered questions tugged at her thoughts, intensifying her longing for understanding. Eventually, exhaustion claimed her, and she succumbed to sleep, her mind still entangled in a web of uncertainties.

The following day held something unexpected. While Emily played in her room, the laughter and chatter of the neighborhood children echoed outside her house, filling the air with a contagious exuberance. From her bedroom window, she watched their games with a mixture of longing and trepidation, feeling like an outsider peering into a world where she didn't quite belong.

One afternoon, as Emily continued her window watching, Jimmy, a boy who lived up the street, glanced her way.

Catching sight of her silhouette through the glass, he waved and called out, "Hey, Emily! Come play kickball with us!"

Emily gave a dismissive wave, her shyness and self-doubt acting as invisible shackles.

Undeterred, Jimmy clambered up to her balcony and stood face-to-face with her through the window. His eyes twinkled with excitement as he said, "C'mon, we need another player."

His earnestness and welcoming smile melted Emily's icy resistance.

"All right, Jimmy," she replied, her voice softer than usual. "You've convinced me. I'm in."

Observing her descent from the house, Scott rolled his eyes and let out a loud groan. "Well, whoever gets stuck with her is definitely going to lose," he muttered, ensuring Emily could hear his disparaging remark.

Her shyness still nagging at her, Emily squared her shoulders, determined to prove herself.

Ignoring Scott's remark, she shot back, "Maybe I'll surprise you, Scott."

A defiant smile graced her lips as she headed toward the others, determined to prove herself in the game.

Scott chuckled and shook his head. "We'll see," he replied, his attention shifting back to the game, a hint of amusement tugging at his mouth.

Jimmy and Scott took on the roles of team captains, selecting their players one by one. Emily, accustomed to being overlooked, braced herself for the inevitable. However, to her utter surprise, Jimmy, his eyes gleaming with mischievous defiance, called out her name much earlier than she had expected. His unexpected selection ignited a spark of confidence within her, dispelling her lingering insecurities.

With the teams assembled, the tranquil park transformed into a vibrant battleground. Cheers erupted as the rubber ball arced through the sky, resembling a launched artillery shell. The competition ignited with raw intensity.

Jimmy, an agile and seasoned player, kicked the ball with such force that it soared through the air, leaving onlookers awestruck. Scott, on the other hand, displayed defensive wizardry, his eyes scanning the field, predicting the ball's trajectory, and skillfully catching any pop-ups that came his way. Their ability turned the game into an adrenaline-pumped spectacle.

Emily, a novice in this boisterous arena, gave her best effort, even though her attempts were at times clumsy. Her foot made half-hearted connections with the ball, causing it to trickle off in the wrong direction. On the defensive, she mistimed a catch, and the ball bounced off her fingertips. With each fumble, a blush crept up her neck, but the embarrassment was overshadowed by the sheer joy of being part of the game.

What Emily lacked in technical ability, she compensated for with enthusiasm. As the minutes passed, self-consciousness waned, and she became fully engaged. To her own surprise, she managed to score a run through a wild kick that sent the ball veering unpredictably past the bewildered players.

The day became truly memorable through the liberating sound of her own laughter, which bubbled up freely. It appeared from deep within her, inspired by spontaneous jokes, comedic blunders, friendly banter, and the simple joy of being included. Her heart felt lighter than it had in a while, the cheer permeating her being and lifting her spirits.

For the first time, Emily wasn't merely seeing life from her window; she was living it, basking in the camaraderie forged through competition, and most importantly, discovering the intoxicating thrill of belonging.

As the game wound down and the teams began to disperse, Emily's chest heaved, her clothes sticky with sweat, but a genuine smile illuminated her face. She was flushed from exertion and excitement, the afternoon sunlight dancing in her eyes.

Just then, Jimmy approached her with a boyish grin. There was a glint in his eyes that conveyed the mutual respect that had developed over the course of the game. Playfully, he landed a light punch on Emily's shoulder, an action that somehow felt like a trophy.

"Good job," he said, his voice carrying a note of sincerity.

He didn't say much more, but his words, coupled with the encouraging smile that spread across his face, were enough. They served as an acknowledgment of her efforts and a warm welcome into the group. As he walked away, leaving Emily standing in the gradually emptying field, the corners of his mouth were still curled up in a smile that promised more afternoons of games and laughter. Approaching them, Scott directed his gaze towards Emily, holding it for a brief moment.

With a dismissive tone, he muttered, "Whatever," before deliberately turning away and walking off.

Jimmy couldn't help but burst into laughter, the sound echoing through the street and lifting her spirits. A genuine smile spread across her face. He walked Emily home, their silence fostering a comforting sense of friendship.

When they arrived at her door, Jimmy turned to her. "Hope you play again."

His words lingered in the air, carrying a sense of anticipation and the promise of more shared moments. She nodded, her own smile mirroring his, as she said goodbye and went inside.

A couple of days later, Jimmy visited Emily. He skillfully scaled the balcony beneath her window, gripping the railing with practiced ease. Softly, he tapped on the glass.

"Hey Emily, do you want to hang out?" his voice carried with the breeze.

A smile graced her face.

"Sure," excitement tingled in her voice. She climbed through the window, her heart pounding with anticipation.

Together, they took a leisurely stroll toward the community stables. As they approached, the air filled with the faint scent of hay and the earthy aroma of horses. The rhythmic sound of hooves echoed in the distance.

When they arrived, they saw Scott and his friends gathered around, expertly fitting a saddle onto her father's horse, 'Trouble.' The powerful stallion exuded an air of defiance, his muscles rippling beneath his glossy cream-colored coat. The boys had agreed to ride the stallion for as long as they could hold on.

Curiosity piqued, Jimmy watched the scene with a mixture of intrigue and trepidation. The unease crackled in the air, thick with excitement and competition.

Scott turned to him, a mischievous glint in his eye, and posed a question, his voice laced with a challenge. "What about you? Do you want to give it a try?"

Jimmy cocked his head, fixing his gaze on the spirited horse in front of him. The breeze played with his hair, carrying the scent of adventure and challenge.

"Is that a dare?" he asked, playful determination in his eyes.

A knowing smile spread across Scott's face, igniting a spark of resolve within Jimmy. Without hesitation, he approached the horse, and in one fluid motion, he hoisted himself onto its back.

In an instant, Trouble erupted into a flurry of motion. Muscles flexed beneath him as the horse galloped with unrestrained power, hooves pounding the ground. Jimmy clung to the saddle with a fierce grip, fully engaged in the exhilarating chaos.

Laughter erupted from Scott and his friends, their voices mingling with the crashing of hooves and the rush of wind. Dust billowed around them, swirling in the air as Jimmy fought to keep his balance. The scent of earth and sweat filled his nostrils, intensifying the moment.

"Go, Jimmy!" they laughed.

After a valiant effort, his grip slipped, and he tumbled from the horse's back, landing in a cloud of dust. Applause and laughter filled the air as he rose to his feet, heart racing and a triumphant smile gracing his lips. The experience had been an adrenaline-fueled adventure, etching itself into his memory.

"Well, maybe you aren't as big a pussy as we thought," Scott laughed.

Jimmy brushed off the dust, exchanging knowing glances with Scott. Taking Emily's hand, he led her to the stables where they discovered a soft pile of hay and settled down. Before she knew what was happening, without hesitation, he reached for Emily's shirt buttons, prompting her to slap his hand.

"What are you doing?" she asked as she pushed his hands away.

Determined, he looked at her, then tried to reach for her blouse again. She forcefully pushed him away. In an aggressive act, he pulled her shirt off her back and began kissing her, while her screams seemed to take over the barn and her mind faded away as she mentally detached herself from the situation.

When she opened her eyes, she found her brother Scott standing over her, his gaze fixed on her.

"Disgusting," he muttered.

Hurriedly, she covered herself and rushed home, seeking refuge in her bedroom. Later, when Scott returned home, his knuckles were bruised and bloodied. He cast a look of revulsion at Emily before retreating to his own room.

Scott harbored a peculiar fascination with snakes, a hobby that manifested itself in a macabre display in their backyard. He expertly caught the serpents, his hands steady despite the danger. Then he skinned them with a precision that belied his tender age, before pinning the sloughed skins onto boards for display. The backyard, under his influence, morphed into an unsettling exhibition of his unsettling pastime.

Steeped as they were in the culture of hunting, Emily's parents viewed Scott's peculiar interest in snakes with a sense of detached normality. Their backyard often bore the weight of dressed deer strung between the trees. Even the children were integrated into this lifestyle, handed the larynx from the prey to fiddle with, a strange plaything akin to a Chinese finger toy.

Against this backdrop of visceral exposure, Scott's snake skinning hardly raised an eyebrow. Their world, framed by the hunt, cast a different hue over activities that might otherwise be considered unusual or disconcerting. This was their normal, the unique tapestry of their life, woven with the strands of their shared interests and experiences.

One afternoon, as the sun dipped toward the horizon, casting golden beams of light through the trees, Emily found herself standing in the shallow pond near the edge of the woods. Scott had dragged her against her will to the pond across the street from their house. He demanded that she stand in the water to attract the attention of the snakes while he killed them with his compound bow.

"Just do it! Either get in, or I'll shoot at you instead," Scott threatened. "Remember, Emily, they're more scared of you than you are of them!"

He nudged her with the compound bow he had received as a gift from his parents. He continued to taunt her as she hesitated. She held her breath and stepped into the water.

Annoyed, Scott shouted, "Stand still! You're going to scare them away!"

While the copperheads encircled and slithered around her, his laughter filled the air. He took sadistic pleasure in her pain. "You're such a piece of shit."

Emily's heart hammered in her chest as she watched the snakes, their sleek bodies coiling and writhing in the murky water. Scott sneered. "Look at you, trembling like a baby deer. It's just a bunch of snakes!"

Her entire body trembled, her breath coming in shallow gasps as she tried to remain as motionless as possible, hoping that the snakes would leave her alone. Suddenly, the whooshing sound of arrows pierced the air, making Emily inch in fright. Her brother had brought his bow and was firing arrows into the water, further agitating the snakes and intensifying Emily's fear. He laughed and taunted her, delighting in her distress as the arrows penetrated the water mere inches from her quivering shoulders.

With a smirk, Scott jeered, "Ha! That was close, wasn't it?"

As Emily's fear threatened to engulf her, she caught sight of the man skulking in the trees, watching the scene unfold with gratification. His presence only heightened her sense of panic, making her feel cornered and powerless, unable to flee the horror that enveloped her. As the man watched the scene unfold, his lips twisted into an amused smile, and he let out a low chuckle.

She closed her eyes and tried to slip away. But her fear was too intense. Her concentration was shattered by the turmoil around her. She couldn't find the solace she so desperately craved. Just when Emily thought she could endure no more, her brother finally ceased firing and waded into the water to grab her arm, yanking her out of the pond. He snickered and ridiculed her as she stumbled onto the shore, her clothes soaked and her body quaking.

As he released her arm, Scott said with a twisted smile, "You should thank me, you know. I'm the reason you're not snake food right now."

Emily couldn't restrain her tears as she sprinted home, her brother's laughter reverberating in her ears. Scott's laughter followed her as he called after her, "Let's do this again tomorrow, snake girl!"

That night, Emily's sleep was fitful. Her dreams were swallowed by the man's presence. As she tossed and turned in her small bed, she struggled to escape the nightmare, but there was no respite from the darkness that had enveloped her life. An oppressive silence descended upon Emily's room, interrupted only by the faint rustle of her bed sheets.

Suddenly, she sensed a presence in the room, a malevolent force that sent ice through her veins. Her eyes flew open, and her heart pounded in her chest as she realized that the man had come for her.

"What do you want?" Emily thought to herself. "Why are you here?"

Paralyzed by fear, she lay motionless in her bed, unable to move or cry out for help. She could feel the man's presence drawing nearer. An asphyxiating weight seemed to bear down on her chest, making it difficult to breathe. As he leaned over her, she could feel his frigid breath on her neck, and his coarse hand stroked her leg. It was a nauseating touch that made her want to scream. But she knew that she couldn't let the man know she was awake and aware of his presence.

The man sensed her consciousness and whispered maliciously, "You're awake, aren't you?" He covered her mouth with his palm. "Be quiet," he hissed. "You'd better not tell anyone I was here. They wouldn't believe you anyway." He gave a mean chuckle. "Don't worry, Emily. It'll be our secret."

He was right. She knew that she couldn't depend on her family to save her, that no one would believe her if she revealed what was happening. The man's words lingered in her mind, a harsh whisper in the silent room. "No one will believe you anyway."

She squeezed her eyes shut and forced herself to run away in her mind. Concentrating, she felt her body grow lighter as she slipped away from the horrifying reality of the man's closeness. She clung to her imaginary haven, praying it would be enough to shield her from the terror that had infiltrated her room.

Finally, the man finished his work and slipped out, vanishing into the shadows. As the door clicked shut behind him, Emily felt her body return to the safety of her bed, the residual chill of his touch still searing her skin.

She murmured to herself in the empty room, "He's gone."

In the days that followed, Emily kept her encounter with the man a secret, fearing that no one would believe her if she told them the truth. She felt more isolated than ever, her nightmares growing more vivid and intense as she grappled with the knowledge that the man could reach her even in her own home.

In a rare moment of spontaneity, Jack exclaimed, "How about a waterskiing trip this weekend?"

The family brimmed with excitement, swiftly gathering their equipment, hitching the boat to the car, and embarking on their journey to the lake. They reveled in the exhilaration of waterskiing, taking turns slicing through the serene surface of the lake. Surprisingly, Scott was filled with uncharacteristic joy.

As the hours of fun unfolded, Jack dropped anchor in the tranquil depths of the lake, intending to fish with Alexandra. However, their tranquility was abruptly disrupted. The calm waters churned suddenly, and the once-blue heavens transformed into a mournful shade of gray. Urgently, Jack beckoned everyone back to the boat, only to discover that it refused to cooperate. Frustration surged within him as the weather worsened and the shore seemed to drift farther away.

"Stand up straight!" Jack told Emily and Scott, his voice authoritative and stern.

They obediently fell in line, their eyes wide and their bodies tense with anticipation. With swift and precise movements, Jack secured thick, coarse ropes around their small waists, ensuring they would not come loose. With a single push, he propelled them into the cold, biting lake, creating a flurry of bubbles around their sun-warmed skin.

"Swim!" he shouted, his voice cutting through the turbulent air.

The icy water shocked their bodies, its once-inviting touch now resembling a thousand tiny needles against their skin. Gasping for breath, they thrashed their arms against the aggressive current, battling the relentless waves that grew higher with each gust of wind.

"Oh, look at them go!" he chuckled, a sense of amusement clear in his voice.

Alexandra's laughter danced across the water, unable to deny the absurdity of the scene unfolding before them. Their children, tied to the boat, resembled two little outboard motors as their legs churned the foamy water with determined kicks. Emily and Scott kicked fiercely, their muscles straining as they worked in unison to propel the boat toward the safety of the shore.

The sudden change in weather and the unexpected malfunction of the boat raced their hearts, yet they knew expressing their fears would only worsen the situation. Tears mixed with the spray of the lake, streaming down Scott's face.

"Quit whining and move it!" Jack's voice boomed from the boat, adding a touch of urgency to their efforts.

Though seemingly impossible, with each resolute kick and desperate stroke, they gradually gained ground against the relentless water, inching closer to the approaching shore. Finally, Jack leaped into the water as it grew shallow. Swiftly, he untied the ropes that had tethered Emily and Scott. Alexandra handed towels to both children, trying to console them.

"Stop crying. It's over now," Alexandra uttered, her patience worn thin by the ordeal.

Unbeknownst to them, a stranger silently watched the spectacle from a hidden spot. Emily's instincts tingled, alerting her to his presence. Upon reaching the shore, Emily's gaze roamed the landscape until it locked onto him.

Time stood still. Emily felt rooted in place, consumed by apprehension. The man, hidden yet fixated on her, exuded an unsettling aura. His smile and nod sent shivers down her spine as if deriving perverse satisfaction from her unease.

Her heart pounded in her chest, each beat echoing a thunderous reminder of the danger she faced. Locked in his gaze, a chilling certainty gripped Emily, conveying that he held an inexplicable power over her. Fear clutched her like a vice.

With no escape and no one to confide in, Emily fled to the back seat of the car, seeking refuge and safety. In the confined space, she silently prayed to God, beseeching protection from the looming threat that haunted her.

Overwhelmed and fatigued, Emily drifted into an uneasy sleep. When she awoke the following morning, disoriented and groggy, she found herself tucked in her own bed. Confusion clouded her thoughts as she struggled to piece together the events of the previous night. A lingering fear gnawed at her, leaving her unsettled.

Weeks went by, and Emily had not seen the man since he invaded her bedroom. She found herself settling into a comforting routine, her mind began to toy with the possibility that the unsettling figure might have been nothing more than a trick of her overactive imagination, a phantom born from her own fears.

One evening, Jack left on a business trip for the weekend, his absence lifting the weight of his domineering presence from their home. Her mother's liveliness permeated the house, infusing it with newfound vitality. It felt as if a burden had been lifted, creating space for mirth to thrive in their lives.

That evening, Alexandra spontaneously suggested a game night. Emily, Alexandra, and Scott gathered in the living room, their laughter harmonizing with the aroma of freshly made popcorn.

"All right, everyone! Get ready for serious game time," Emily's mother declared with a mischievous smile.

Emily joined in, her eyes sparkling with excitement. "What's the first game, Mom?"

Her mother chuckled. "How about a classic? Let's start with charades!"

The room erupted with eager agreement as they settled into their places, ready to enjoy an evening of friendly competition. As the game unfolded, their laughter became the soundtrack of their time together, punctuated by enthusiastic guesses and hilarious gestures.

Emily mimicked an iconic scene from a famous movie, while Scott and Alexandra frantically tried to decipher her actions, their faces contorted in confusion and amusement.

"I've got it! You're reenacting 'The Aristocats!'" Scott exclaimed, causing everyone to burst into laughter.

Emily nodded, a wide grin spreading across her face. "You nailed it!"

The game continued, with each member of the family taking turns and immersing themselves in the challenge of portraying different characters and scenarios. The room echoed with their uproarious laughter, creating an atmosphere of pure bliss and camaraderie.

For Emily, the chains of loneliness gradually loosened, the oppressive gloom retreating, and a buoyant lightness took its place. She surrendered herself to the moment.

The day after their game night, Emily walked to school alone because Scott had come down with a sudden fever. Her pace was slower than her schoolmates' because she took comfort in the joys that nature offered. She gathered the smooth stones and frail blossoms that graced her path.

Engrossed in a private daydream, she bent over to pluck a dandelion. From the corner of her eye, she noticed a car creeping up behind her with an unnerving slowness. Emily's heart missed a beat when she turned around to discover a man motioning her to come closer. Instinct propelled her into a run, her legs working fervently to carry her far away. But she lost her balance at the road's edge and stumbled into a ditch. She hit the bottom with a startling impact. Lying dazed and breathless, she stared up at the sky.

As the kicked-up dust settled, Emily spotted the man standing at the crest of the slope, a strange smile etched onto his face. An icy shiver trickled down her spine; a silent scream urged her to rise and flee. Gathering her strength, she hoisted herself up, cast a final, frightened look at him, and bolted for her school. She arrived breathless and disheveled.

Her teacher greeted her with a reproachful stare that cut down Emily's already diminutive self-esteem. "Late again. Go to the restroom and clean up."

With a silent nod, Emily complied, wanting to remove any signs of her ordeal.

In the restroom, she carefully washed her hands, which quaked as she tidied her tousled hair and brushed the grime off her clothes. When she was done, she made her way back to the classroom, slipping quietly into her seat, hoping her classmates were too engrossed in their work to notice her unkempt appearance. In the still depths of her chest, trepidation spread and coiled around her mind. He had returned.

Emily grew increasingly desperate to escape her situation. She muttered to herself, "I'll find a way... I'll find a way out of this." She realized that her hidden world could no longer provide her with the protection she needed. The man had found a way to breach her safety. Resolved to be outside his reach, Emily decided to flee to the woods. She believed that the vast expanse of trees and the refuge of the forest would afford her a chance of freedom, a place where she could hide from the nightmares that tormented her.

The following Saturday, Emily packed a small bag with her most cherished belongings, leaving behind a note for her parents explaining her decision. With a heavy heart, she slipped out of her house and into the darkness, the moon illuminating her path as she ventured deeper into the woods.

As she walked through the forest, she felt a sense of hope and determination grow within her. She believed that she could evade the man, that she could create a new life for herself, free from the shadow of his malevolent influence. "You won't find me. You won't get me," she whispered to herself, a determined glint in her eyes.

As the hours passed and the forest darkened, she began to feel a familiar sense of disquiet crawl over her. The silence of the woods was disrupted by the rustle of leaves and the snap of twigs, the eerie sounds weakening her knees.

Suddenly, she spotted a figure standing in the shadows, watching her from the perimeter of a clearing.

Emily's heart raced as she recognized that the man had found her, and she whimpered, "Not again!"

Panic surged within her, and she began running, her breath coming in short, desperate gasps as she tried to distance herself from the man. The forest became a blur of shadows and moonlight as she sprinted through the trees, her legs aching and her lungs burning with exertion.

In her haste, she did not see the exposed root in her path and tripped, falling hard onto the forest floor. A sharp pain coursed through her leg as a jagged rock tore through her skin.

"Damn it!" Blood streamed down her calf as she struggled to stand.

Despite the pain, she forced herself to continue, driven by an overwhelming need to escape the man's grasp. With every step, her desperation intensified.

Fear and adrenaline propelled her to run faster and harder than she ever had before.

The man was on top of her when Old Man Fear stepped out of the shadows.

Emily cried out, "Please, no!"

He was wearing a tattered shirt and torn pants. In the storm, he looked like a giant.

With surprisingly quick actions, he stepped between Emily and the man.

"Get behind me!"

She was terrified of him, but she was more terrified of the man chasing her, so she did as she was told. The two men stood face to face, silently threatening one another. Finally, the man left. Old Man Fear turned around and placed a hand on her shoulder.

"Go home," he said. It was the first time she realized that he had kind eyes.

She stammered, "Thank you... I... thank you."

He followed her from a distance and stood watch while she found the edge of the neighborhood. She turned to wave goodbye, but he was gone.

She burst out of the woods and stumbled onto the familiar path that led to her home. Her clothes were filthy, her body bruised and bloodied, but she didn't care. All that mattered was putting as much distance between herself and the man as possible.

When she arrived home, her mother was waiting. Her face was a mix of worry and anger. As she tried to explain what had happened, her voice quivered, and her eyes filled with tears.

Emily's mother refused to believe her, convinced that she had fabricated the entire ordeal.

"Stop making up stories. You've always been so dramatic lately," she said.

She responded to her mother's disbelief with frustration, saying, "Why don't you believe me? This isn't a story! I swear I saw him. He's been following me!"

Frustration and despair welled up inside her as she was taken to the bathroom to be cleaned. Her mother's disbelief cut like a knife into her heart. As the warm water washed away the grime and the blood, Emily felt lonelier than ever, the weight of her secret fears and the man's presence bearing down on her.

She was sent to bed, her thoughts swirling with fear. The man had proven that there was nowhere she could hide, no sanctuary that could shield her from his relentless pursuit. She knew that she would have to find the strength within herself to confront her fears and protect her family, but the path ahead seemed darker and more perilous than ever before.

Emily lay in her bed, the events of the previous night replaying incessantly in her mind. The man's pursuit through the woods, the disbelief in her mother's eyes, and the feeling of helplessness that threatened to engulf her weighed heavily on her heart.

In the days that followed, she grew increasingly anxious.

Muttering under her breath, she pleaded, "Just leave me alone... please." She felt the man's presence intensifying, a constant weight that hung over her like a dark cloud.

One night, as she played with her toys in her room, she felt a sudden chill in the air. The room grew eerily silent, and the familiar sense of dread began to fill her chest. She knew, without a doubt, that the man had come.

Desperate to escape, Emily tried to hide in one of her secret worlds, squeezing her eyes shut. But it didn't work.

The man seemed to obstruct her escape, trapping her in the horrifying reality of his pursuit.

As he stepped into the light, his chilling gaze locked onto Emily's trembling form.

She cried out defiantly, "I won't go with you."

She could feel the terror coursing through her veins, her heart pounding in her chest like a caged bird.

With a final, desperate burst of strength, she tried to flee, running toward the door in a last-ditch effort to escape her tormentor. But the man was too fast, his chilling grip closing around her arm, preventing her escape.

"Let go of me!" Emily shrieked, fear and desperation filling her voice.

Emily struggled against his grasp. Fear and panic surged through her as she tried to break free. But the man's grip was unyielding. His smile was a promise of the darkness that awaited her. As her strength began to wane, Emily's thoughts raced, searching for a way to escape her fate.

In that final, desperate moment, Emily realized she had only one choice remaining. As the man's grip tightened around her arm, she closed her eyes and focused all her energy, channeling every ounce of her fear, her hope, and her determination into her imagination, willing herself to slip away.

As she concentrated, the man's presence seemed to fade, his grip slowly losing its strength. Emily felt herself being pulled away, her body shrinking and shrinking until she vanished completely.

The next morning, Emily's mother sent her brother to wake her up for breakfast. As Scott entered her room, he paused for a moment, taking in the eerie silence that filled the space.

"What are you doing? Get the fuck up! Mom wants you to get your butt up for breakfast." He stood motionless, waiting. Then, in a panicked voice, he cried out, "Mom!"

Casting long shadows on the neatly trimmed grass, the house at the end of the lane was a testament to a past that refused to fade. The immaculately painted wooden façade, once an emblem of joy, now held only the lingering memories of a family torn apart by tragedy.

Weathered by time and heartache that never seemed to subside, Jack held steadfast onto the home he once shared with his ex-wife and their two children. Every scratch on the wooden floors and every smudge on the windowpanes held a record of Emily's laughter. The house was a ghostly reminder of the happy child who had once graced their lives. But Alexandra couldn't bear the weight of those burdensome memories, and the house felt like a tombstone to her. Their shared grief turned into an insurmountable barrier in their relationship, and she chose to leave.

It had been ten years since Emily's disappearance. A poignant red circle on the wall calendar marked the anniversary. The entire community came together each year bearing flowers, photos, and silent prayer in a communal act of remembering. They honored the bright-eyed girl who had once played in their streets, now reduced to a memory.

Scott, now in his mid-twenties, lived with his father. His once-youthful face was shadowed with guilt and remorse, reflecting a pain far beyond his years. The loss of Emily was a wound that festered within him, gnawing at his spirit and feeding on his guilt. He was the last person to see her on that ill-fated day, and he blamed himself, a self-imposed punishment for a crime he didn't commit.

When Alexandra arrived at the gathering, her face was a mask of stoic sorrow. There was an uncomfortable pause when Jack walked up to her. Their eyes met. It had been a year without communication.

She glanced at Scott, her heart aching. His eyes reflected the loss she felt every waking day.

"Scott," she whispered, pulling him into a tight embrace, "it's not your fault."

But Scott could only nod. His guilt was a monster that refused to be tamed. Jack placed a hand on his shoulder. There was an unspoken bond between them, a promise that they would be in this together.

That night, as the lanterns floated into the night sky—each a symbol of a memory, a wish, a prayer for Emily—the family stood together, united in loss. They shed tears and shared stories. Jack, Alexandra, and Scott found solace in this act of remembering. The collective memory of Emily was a beacon guiding them through their darkest hour. Jack stood alone, staring at the ascending lights with a faraway look in his eyes.

As the lanterns ascended toward the heavens, a faint silhouette lingered at the edge of the gathering, just out of the reach of the flickering streetlights. A shadowy figure hidden under the brim of a low-set hat watched the scene with an intense, calculating gaze. His eyes, piercing through the semi-darkness, never strayed far from the Wilson family.

His interest would have been unsettling if anyone had noticed his presence. But he was like a ghost, invisible to the grieving crowd. His posture held a certain tension and a purpose cloaked beneath anonymity. He had the air of someone who had purposefully distanced himself, physically and emotionally, as if the chasm of years were a protective barrier against a past he'd rather not touch.

As the last lantern floated away, becoming a tiny speck against the vast inkiness of the night sky, the man turned away from the scene, his eyes having recorded every detail of the grieving family. After one final glance, he turned and walked away. Satisfaction played at the corners of his mouth, turning into a chuckle that was part triumph and part resolution.

The Unrelenting